The Scheming Mr Cleeve

By the same author

TENDER DECEPTION

ISLAND FOR FIONA

ROMANCE IN RAVENDALE

HAUNTED BY SANDRA

HEARTBREAK AT HAVERSHAM

WAITING FOR MATT

MISTRESS OF CALVERLEY

A DISGRACEFUL DECEIT

A WAYWARD MISS

The Scheming Mr Cleeve

Gillian Kaye

ROBERT HALE · LONDON

First published in Great Britain 2001

ISBN 0 7090 6793 3

Robert Hale Limited
Clerkenwell House
Clerkenwell Green
London EC1R 0HT

2 4 6 8 10 9 7 5 3 1

Typeset by
Derek Doyle & Associates, Liverpool.
Printed in Great Britain by
St Edmundsbury Press Ltd, Bury St Edmunds, Suffolk.
Bound by Woolnough Bookbinders Ltd

One

IT WAS NOT in Sarah Winterson's nature to have either bad-tempered or flustered freaks but that spring morning at Cleeve Grange in Kent, she suffered both in the space of a few minutes.

The family was moving house and her mother, Lady Hadlow, and her sister, Marianne, together with the maids, had gone on before her in the carriage to try and make themselves comfortable in the small steward's house they were to rent in the grounds of the Grange.

Sarah had stayed on at the Grange to gather up oddments of their belongings which had been left behind and to straighten the house without the help of a maid. And, as if this was all not enough to vex her and to overturn both her spirits and her temper, she was suddenly faced with an obstinate Mrs Lingfield. This good and rather large woman had been the Cleeve Grange cook for as long as Sarah could remember and Sarah was four-and-twenty years of age.

And now here was the beloved and faithful Mrs Lingfield standing astride in the kitchen and positively refusing to move to such a paltry house as Little Cleeve.

Sarah was trying to listen to Mrs Lingfield's grievances with patience, but when her ear caught the sound of wheels on the gravel at the front of the house and heard the heavy knocking at the front door, she lost her temper. And then she shouted at the astonished Mrs Lingfield who had only ever known a kind, yet rather high-spirited and managing, Miss Sarah.

'A morning caller and today of all days,' grumbled Sarah. 'Who can possibly be so thoughtless when everyone in the district knows that we are removing to Little Cleeve today . . . no, stay there, Mrs Lingfield. I will have to answer the door myself and whoever it is will get short shrift from me, I can tell you.'

Sarah was a tall, dark girl; she was considered handsome rather than beautiful, with fine eyes of deep brown in a face of strong features. Her expression was usually lively and sympathetic if somewhat sensible. She always dressed neatly, but never in style and today was no exception; her morning dress of a stout fawn cotton was crumpled and dirty, and her hair, usually gathered high on her head, was wispy and untidy.

When she opened the door and found herself facing not only a complete stranger but the most handsome man she had ever met, she found herself speechless.

In one glance, she took in the fashionable curricle standing in the drive, the magnificence of the visitor's riding-coat with its several capes and the classic features of a man with hair as dark as her own. He stood there with an expression of hauteur which was tempered by the look of amusement in his eyes.

'Lady Hadlow, if you please.' The request came in a voice both smooth and superior.

He thinks I am the maid, thought Sarah, and all the frustrations of the morning boiled to the surface and she was intolerably rude.

'No, I am not the maid and my mother, Lady Hadlow, is no longer here. She has been turned out of her home by a wretched cousin in America and has suffered the indignity of having to move into the lodge which is much too small for a family. If you wish to speak to her, you will find her there – down the drive and to the right. But I had better warn you that you will not be made welcome as she is suffering from a severe shock to the nerves – not to say a fit of the dismals – at having to leave her home. Good morning.'

And she shut the door in his face and stalked back towards the kitchen knowing that she had been more impolite than she had ever been in her life.

But she did not reach the kitchen, as the front door was opened behind her and she heard a cool voice.

'Ma'am, I apologize for mistaking you for a servant and I can understand your loss of composure, but you did not ask my name.'

Sarah turned to meet a piercing gaze from eyes which were unusually grey under such dark hair and which held an expression both of anger and what seemed to be an offended amusement.

'I have no wish to know your name,' she replied, still cattish. 'You are obviously a stranger to the neighbourhood and at the moment I have my hands full with the move to Little Cleeve. Not only that, our cook is refusing to come with us; she has been cook all her life at Cleeve Grange and says she will continue to cook for our abominable cousin if he wishes to keep her on.'

'I am your abominable cousin.'

They were standing in the large and imposing entrance hall of the Grange which was lacking many of its cabinets and small tables. Lady Hadlow had taken them to help furnish Little Cleeve.

So the stranger's words dropped into a hollow, empty silence as Sarah stared at him. She took a step towards him, unbelieving and very shocked.

'Would you mind saying that again?' Her voice came as a hoarse whisper.

His expression did not change, his tone was sardonic. 'I am your abominable cousin.' He saw a variety of emotions cross her face which had a black smudge on the forehead and he thought she looked charmingly young. Then he spoke again. 'I am Julian Cleeve.'

Sarah felt her heart thump in her astonishment and embarrassment; she felt bewildered at the sight of a young man of high fashion, and she had a horrid remembrance of her rudeness to him when she had opened the door. So her words refused to be reasoned or even calm.

'But you cannot be. Cousin Julian is older than my mother and she is in her fortieth year. We had a letter from him saying that he wanted to come back and live at Cleeve Grange. That is why we are moving down to the lodge.'

For the first time, the visitor lost his top-lofty look and his face took on a more amicable expression. 'I believe you must be one of my cousins even if you do look like the maid and you answered my knock on the door. Is there somewhere we can sit and I will explain the matter to you?'

Sarah could think of only two things: it was her mother's cousin in America who was the owner of Cleeve Grange and who was turning them out; this must be his son and she had been unbelievably rude to him.

All she did was to turn and open a door off the hall. 'Come into the drawing-room, we will be private there.'

He followed her into the gracious room and they sat facing each other on either side of the fireplace though no fire had been lit that morning.

Sarah was the first to speak and she felt the humiliation of having to apologize for her behaviour. 'I am sorry, I took you for a casual visitor. It is a very difficult day for us having to leave our home and I am not in the best of humours.'

'And I caught the sharp edge of your tongue?' He continued to sound more approachable, but she could not begin to consider him with any favour.

'Your father – I assume it was your father – has turned us out of the only house we have ever known and we are all feeling miserable. It is not usual for me to lose my temper quite so forcibly, but I do not feel charitably towards your family.' Sarah knew that her voice was full of the stiff resentment she was feeling but she could not bring herself to be amiable.

The man who said he was Julian Cleeve looked at her. 'May I correct you on two points? My father died last year and I am now the owner of Cleeve Grange, that is the first thing. The second, is that I must remind you that the house never belonged to your family. Your father was glad to move into it at what I consider to be a ridiculously low rent when he was out of funds due to his gaming habits.' He stopped speaking and looked at her keenly across the fireplace. 'There, now I have been equally rude to you so we are on the same terms and perhaps can converse in a civilized manner . . . and may I tell you that you have a black smudge on your forehead which is quite fetching. Would you allow me to remove it for you?'

Sarah flushed scarlet and started to rise from her chair. 'You are detestable. As if I am not in enough trouble already without being reminded that I have a dirty face.'

But his hand was on her arm and urging her back into her chair; he had his handkerchief in his hand and a smile in his expression which infuriated her still further.

'Stay still,' he commanded.

His fingers rubbed hard at the dirty spot then he showed her the white square of his handkerchief which indeed had the proof of the grime on her forehead.

'Thank you,' she said stiffly. 'I expect my hair is untidy as well. Would you like to put it in place for me?' Sarah was horrified at her impertinence, but found it impossible to be civil to this handsome, overbearing stranger.

'I do not think that even my skills would run to arranging a lady's hair,' he replied smoothly. 'Now do you think you could forget the injuries caused to you by my family and talk sensibly for a little while?'

'I am not feeling at all sensible, but I will have to try. How is it that we did not know of our cousin's death?'

'My father suffered a short illness, but was able to tell me his wishes before he died. It had never been his intention to take up residence in England again, but he wanted me to find out what was happening over here. I must tell you . . . dammit, I do not even know your name.'

'I am Sarah Winterson – the Honorable Sarah Winterson to be exact – and I am the eldest in the family. My father, Robert Winterson, the third Baron Hadlow, died just over three years ago and his finances were in a sad state; but we have a good friend and lawyer, Mr Lumley, of Tunbridge Wells, who has handled our affairs for us. I have been able to leave all our financial matters in his hands while I attended to the running of the estate. My mother is rather a poor creature, I regret to say, easily overcome. She feels the loss of her husband sadly. My younger sister, Marianne, should have made her come-out, but it has proved too great an expense as we needed to send to James to Oxford. He wishes to enter the Foreign Office.'

'James?'

'Yes, I am sorry, I should have told you: he is the only Winterson son and is now Lord Hadlow, of course. He is nearly twenty years of age.'

'He is not here to help you move?' It was a quick question.

'No, we did not wish to disturb his studies. We thought we could manage on our own – until this morning, that is. Then Mama broke down completely, the cook gave notice and. . . .' She could not go on.

'I arrived.'

His intervention did not put her into confusion for the sudden softening of his expression eased Sarah's feelings and she gave a rueful smile.

She found she was looking into grey eyes which were not as

steely as they had been on his arrival, and she made up her mind not to treat him with such hostility. 'I am sorry, you did not get a very good reception at the house which must be your home if your father has died. You were telling me why we were not informed of his death.'

Julian Cleeve looked at the young lady who was sitting upright across from him. Here was a girl faced with many difficulties and if she was not exactly beautiful, then her face showed both intelligence and a lurking sense of humour. She could only be described as passably good-looking, but she had a forceful character which was an attraction in itself.

'Father had never told me of the arrangements he had made for Cleeve Grange except that he had let it to a friend who had been in financial straits. Before he died, he let it be known that he had received no rent for over three years after he had been informed of the death of Lord Hadlow. He wished me to come over here and find out what was happening at the Grange and if Lady Hadlow was still living here. It was also his dearest wish that I should take up residence so that there would be a Cleeve once again at the Grange. . . .' He stopped, for he could see shock in the face which already had much to bear.

Sarah found herself stammering, 'But do you mean that Mr Lumley has not paid any rent for us? I know we are sadly purse-pinched but I have relied on him. I was sure he must have had it in hand and I do apologize; it is beyond understanding. We are in your debt then?'

'Do not give it another thought,' he said instantly. 'My father made his fortune in Virginia and, as he spent very little – I am afraid what he did spend was on drink and it was the drink which brought him to his end – it has all passed to me. His greatest concern was not about the money but that Cleeve Grange might be unoccupied and lying in neglect.' He looked around him. 'I can see that he need not have been worried.'

Sarah felt suddenly proud. It was true that the Wintersons had little fortune, but since her father's death she had made sure that the house was well cared for. It showed in the neat hangings, the shine on the furniture, even in the newly embroidered cushions on the chairs.

'I have tried to take care of it,' she confessed, then continued oddly sad, 'and now it is ours no longer. But what am I to do? We are in debt to you and I have no idea how to repay it. I will have to ask Mr Lumley.'

He stood up and walked round the spacious high-ceilinged room; the Grange had been built almost a century before when country houses were gracious, rambling and comfortable. He liked what he saw and looked out of the long windows on to well-kept lawns and a curving drive which swept almost out of view, though he could see a small house as it reached the gates.

'Is that the house you have moved into?' he turned and asked her.

She came and stood beside him. 'Yes, it is called Little Cleeve and it was the steward's lodge at one time. But it is more than a lodge, it has a drawing-room as well as a dining-room and there are four bedrooms with some small attic rooms for the servants. In all honesty, it is quite big enough for the three of us, it is my mother who is feeling rather put down after the grandeur of the Grange. We will come about, Cousin Julian.'

He looked at her closely. 'Would you not like to drop the "cousin"?' he asked lightly.

Her reply came quickly. 'I would prefer to be formal, sir, though we are hardly cousins, are we?'

He gave a short laugh. 'We meet somewhere on the family tree, though it has always been a complicated relationship and one only of marriage, I believe, not of blood.'

'I know the connection,' she said, with a sudden and cheerful remembrance. 'I used to love the story when I was small for it sounded quite romantic, but it is very involved. Mama had a brother who was my Uncle Henry – they came from a very good family you know, but he was a younger son. Uncle Henry married my Aunt Joan and took her off to Virginia to make his fortune, but she refused to go unchaperoned so she took her cousin, Margaret, with her. They sought out your father because he was the only person known to them and then they settled nearby. Cousin Margaret married your father so he became our Cousin Julian after that. My Uncle Henry died and we lost touch with Aunt Joan; I never knew if they had any family. Your father was not a good correspondent so I did not even know that he had a son. . . .' She stopped and gave a little grin. 'I am sorry, I run on. Is your mother still alive?'

He shook his head. 'She died when I was born so I had no brothers and sisters. I was fond of your Uncle Henry, but after he died your Aunt Joan married again and moved west.'

Her next question, which sounded presumptuous, slipped from her before she could stop it.

'You are married?'

He gave a sigh but his expression was not of sadness. 'We had better sit down again and I will explain my reason for wanting to come to England and to live at Cleeve Grange – apart from the wishes of my father, that is.'

Sarah felt curious. She had started off in dislike of the visitor, but he had been courteous and seemingly generous about the lack of rents for the house.

'I will start with my father's death just a year ago. It was my intention to visit England to see if Cleeve Grange would suit me. You must remember that I was born and brought up in America and knew of my father's home only from the stories he told me of his youth. He had been very successful in Virginia and had a spendid plantation; he had no wish to return to England to live but encouraged me to come. . . .' He looked at her serious face. 'I am running on, now!'

'No,' she said instantly, 'it is very interesting.'

He continued, 'When I was eighteen, I met Lucy Terrington who was to become my wife. She was the wealthy daughter of another tobacco planter from the other side of the state, but her family came to live nearby. I was captivated by Lucy. She was beautiful, charming, always laughing; she loved riding. So I married her and our daughter was born a year later . . . I hope I am not boring you, it suddenly seems important that you should know the whole.'

As Sarah was gripped with curiosity by this time, she simply nodded. 'No, do carry on.'

'Our daughter was born a year later and we called her Anita; after that Lucy changed. She did not want to stay at home, she was always out at every entertainment Virginia had to offer. It became obvous that she had married too young and regretted being tied to a husband, a house and a young child. We had a good nanny for Anita so she did not suffer, but I prefer to forget the next few years. After my father died, Lucy refused to come to England with me and in the end, we quarrelled and she went off to live with the man who had been her lover for years. I was just making the final plans to bring Anita over here when two things happened.' He paused for a moment but Sarah did not interrupt.

'First came the news that Lucy had caught a fever and had died; then, within weeks of that happening, Anita was out riding and she had a fall and broke her leg. . . .'

'Oh, I am sorry, you have had a wretched year.' Sarah, her own troubles forgotten, spoke in her usual warm voice of sympathy and friendliness and Julian Cleeve looked at her sharply. He saw the concern in her face and guessed at a caring nature which had been hidden under the bitter words she had spoken on his arrival.

'It has not been easy,' he said slowly, 'but I am hoping for a successful outcome. And I am afraid I must bore you a little more for I would like you to know of my intention in coming to Cleeve

Grange. Anita recovered from her riding accident; her leg mended, but she has been left with a slight limp. She is only eighteen and is very conscious of it and it has made her shy and diffident which is not her true nature at all. If we had stayed in Virginia, she would have had only myself for company and I did not wish for that.' He broke off to see if he still commanded her interest and Sarah gave a slight nod.

'I thought that if I could bring Anita to Cleeve Grange to live, she could enter into society and enjoy some of the entertainments of Tunbridge Wells.' He paused again as he saw a slight frown reach her eyes. 'What are you thinking?'

'It is nothing to do with me, but you would need a chaperon for her, someone to introduce her at the assemblies and balls. . . .' Sarah hesitated, fearing to say the next words. 'And maybe she is not able to dance after her accident.'

'I think she is only lacking in confidence; if she is with other young people, it might encourage her. She might even try riding again, which would be good for her.'

Sarah nodded. 'Where is she at the moment?'

He smiled at her. It was the first time she had seen him smile and it seemed to change him. He was handsome admittedly; straight nose, decisive mouth, strong cheekbones and those clear, grey eyes. But he had preserved a stiffness as though he was on his guard and she had found it off-putting; the smile made him more approachable.

'It is my one piece of good fortune. My father had a friend in Tunbridge Wells and, although they had never corresponded, I was able to find his address. I wrote to him and received a most cordial invitation to visit them if ever I came to Cleeve Grange. That is where Anita is now. Sir Roger Humphries and his wife, Lady Elizabeth, are excellent people and it was Sir Roger who told me that Lady Hadlow had not remarried and still lived at Cleeve Grange. Do you know of them?'

'My father knew Sir Roger,' Sarah replied thoughtfully, 'but their children were older than us Wintersons. Except that I do believe there was a son, Oliver, who was only a little older than me. Then I seem to remember they had a very young daughter. These last few years we have not mixed very much socially.' She added the words defensively.

'But you are quite right. The older children have married and left home; Oliver is a lawyer in London, and Jane is still at home; she is the same age as Anita and the two of them are getting along famously.'

Sarah was thinking hard. Perhaps if her cousin and his daughter came to live at the Grange then it would be company for her younger sister. Marianne was a litle older than Anita and she longed to be in society.

Their nearest village was Bidborough and it was only a short drive to the centre of fashionable Tunbridge Wells; it also lay just off the turnpike road that took them into the heart of London.

'What are you thinking?' Her cousin's voice broke into her thoughts.

'To tell you the truth, 1 was thinking of my sister Marianne. She is close to Anita in age, perhaps they could become friends.'

'Excellent. May I bring Anita to call upon your mother at Little Cleeve? I would like to make sure that you are comfortable.'

'Thank you, perhaps in a few days when Mama is more settled.' Sarah stood up as though she was thinking of something else.

'What is it, Miss Winterson? I can see that something is bothering you.'

But Sarah did not say the words she had intended. 'Would you prefer to call me Sarah? We are almost cousins, after all.'

He gave a chuckle and she liked the sound of it. 'Very well, Sarah, and I will be Julian. But that is not what you were going to say.'

She gave a shake of the head. 'No, I was thinking of Mrs

Lingfield. She is our cook and is refusing to come to Little Cleeve. What are we to do about her?'

'Would you mind if I kept her on? Can you find someone else?' He asked the questions politely.

She looked at him with gratitude. 'You would keep her on? Oh, she would be pleased. Shall we go and ask her? And do not worry about us, one of our parlour-maids, Ellen, has been helping Mrs Lingfield. I was thinking I would have to turn her off now that we are in a much smaller house, but I will ask her if she will cook for us. And Mama would be so pleased for she is fond of Ellen.'

'Admirable,' he said. 'Shall I escort you to the kitchen?'

In the kitchen, Sarah discovered that her cousin Julian could be a charmer if it so pleased him.

Mrs Lingfield was sulking over a pot of coffee when they entered, but jumped up immediately when she saw the visitor.

'Mrs Lingfield,' said Sarah, 'this is my cousin, Mr Julian Cleeve. He has come from America with his daughter and it is his intention to live with Anita at Cleeve Grange.'

'Will you be wanting your own cook then, sir?' asked Mrs Lingfield reluctantly.

In reply, and to Sarah's astonishment, Julian Cleeve shook the cook by the hand. 'Mrs Lingfield, I want no other cook but you for my father told me about you. Father remembered you even though it is over thirty years since he left.'

'Well, would you believe it,' said the good woman with a beaming smile. 'And me only a young girl in my very first place. And when his father died – that would be your grandfather, sir – he wouldn't stay in the place but had to go chasing off to America and letting the house to Lord Hadlow which were a good thing, if I might say so, for they've taken care of the Grange something wonderful. And now poor Lady Hadlow has gone to Little Cleeve, but it had to come one day and she'll be all right with Miss Sarah to look after her.'

Sarah thought she had better interrupt. 'So you will stay with

Mr Cleeve then, Mrs Lingfield?' she asked and felt a glimmer of amusement at the meeting between her cousin and the cook.

'Yes, of course I will, Miss Sarah, and you get that Ellen to cook for your mama. She's a good girl is Ellen.'

'Yes, I was telling Mr Cleeve that I would do just that.'

In the entrance hall once again, Sarah hesitated. 'I did not offer you any refreshment. Will you have a glass of sherry?' she asked her cousin.

'No, thank you, I will return to Tunbridge Wells in a few moments and tell Anita the good news. But first perhaps you would not mind showing me around the house.'

Sarah was proud to do so as she knew it was all in good order even though their personal effects had been removed to Little Cleeve.

By the time she was seeing him off at the front door, Sarah was beginning to lose her resentment at being turned out of the house. She even felt she might come to like its rightful owner though there was something smooth and polished in his manner which seemed to make her hesitate in her good opinion of him.

'Sarah,' said Julian Cleeve, as he held her hand while they stood together on the steps of the porch – she was made very conscious of the strength of his clasp. 'We started off badly but I hope we can be friends. I will give you time to settle into Little Cleeve and then I will bring Anita to call. Please give my regards to your mama and do not hesitate to let me know if there is any way in which I can make her more comfortable.'

'Thank you, Cousin Julian,' Sarah replied, but the words were said rather formally. She watched him drive off and then went back into the house to gather up her travelling-bag which was full of knick-knacks her mother had left behind.

She said goodbye to Mrs Lingfield and promised to send the two youngest maids back and to keep just Ellen and Nancy at Little Cleeve.

Then, the carriage having taken her mother, Marianne and the maids down to Little Cleeve, she set off for a quick walk down the drive. She liked walking and was glad to be out in the fresh air and to have time to think over the events of the morning and of Julian Cleeve in particular.

I was prepared to hate him, she was saying to himself, then I considered him superior and now I am wondering if it might not be to our advantage to have a neighbour who is not only a cousin, but a gentleman of some substance. He has a daughter who would be company for Marianne and it could possibly lead to a season in Tunbridge Wells for the two girls.

And she walked on towards their new home, her thoughts far away. Although it was the spring of 1814, the country was still celebrating the defeat of Napoleon and his exile to the island of Elba.

There are sure to be special balls and assemblies in Tunbridge Wells, Sarah was musing, and perhaps the quieter watering place would suit my cousin Anita better than the rigours of the London season. She might even benefit from the spa waters if she is invalidish as her father suggests.

She tried to keep the thoughts about the unpaid rent at the back of her mind until the time came when she would have to mention the situation to her mother.

Little Cleeve came into sight and Sarah tried to view it dispassionately. Having to move from the Grange had come as such a shock to the family that it felt almost as though they were having to move into squalor.

But here was a solid and handsome stone-built house, ordinary in the placing of its windows and the plain frontage lacking a porch, but it had been built in front of a small copse of trees and its setting seemed to give it an air of pastoral elegance. It also had the advantage of a small stable block with a cottage which just suited Reuben Lunn, who was their coachman, stable boy and gardener all rolled into one. He had been with the family for many years; indeed, Lady Hadlow had brought him with her when she was first married and he was a young lad. Nowadays, not a week went by that one of the Wintersons would say that they did not know what they would do without Reuben to help them.

As she stood quietly looking at the house which was to be her new home, Sarah heard the sound of a horse and a familiar voice calling her name.

'Sarah, wait for a moment.'

She turned with a smile for she knew that the voice belonged to their nearest neighbour, Philip Hesslewood, who lived as a young widower on his own at the dower house of Luttons Park which was owned and occupied by his older brother, Sir Bertram Hesslewood.

Sarah had grown up with the Hesslewood children and Philip being the closest to her in age, had been the constant companion of her early days.

Of Sir Bertram – a full fifteen years older than Philip for there were many married sisters in between them – Sarah preferred not to think at this moment.

Philip Hesslewood jumped down from his horse and stood looking at Sarah, a hand on her arm. 'How are you, Sarah? I came to see if I could help you in the move, but Bertram is already in possession at Little Cleeve trying to comfort his future mama-in-law.'

Sarah was outraged for she knew his meaning. Sir Bertram had been pursuing her for months, trying to persuade her to marry him and she was not best pleased at his efforts.

'Philip, you are outrageous. I have nothing to say to such a wicked remark.' Her eyes met his smiling blue ones and they both laughed. Always on easy terms with Philip, she realized she took for granted how handsome he was.

Now she found herself comparing him with her visitor of the

morning who had so impressed her with his good looks and elegance.

Philip was dressed casually for riding, but he matched her American cousin in looks, for his features were classically handsome and there was no denying his slim grace underneath a blue riding-jacket. He was lithe and strong for he managed the Luttons Park estate for his brother and he looked the epitome of a man used to an outdoor life, far from being the dandy and gracing the drawing-rooms of Tunbridge Wells and the neighbourhood.

He looked at Sarah with great affection; she had always been the close companion and little sister to him for they shared the same interests and he thought he knew her every mood, even the quick, shrewish temper she would show on provocation.

'I thought you were all set to marry Bertram, Sarah, and set up at Luttons Park. Bertram is determined on it, you know.'

'I do know and I have no wish to be reminded of his dogged pursuit of me. He bores me to distraction. How he can possibly be your brother, I fail to understand.'

Philip chuckled. 'I think the only thing we have in common is the name of Hesslewood. You are never going to turn him down, Sarah, it would be a very good match, you know.'

Sarah groaned. 'Please, don't you start on that; it is what Mama is always saying. She is very fond of Bertram.'

'So I have noticed; perhaps they would make a pair and you would be free. I would offer for you myself, but you know that I have vowed never to replace my sweet Clara in my affections.'

Sarah saw the usual sad remembrance in his face; it was always there when he spoke or thought of Clara.

Five years before, when Philip had been four-and-twenty and Sarah only nineteen, Philip had married Clara Wykeham and they had set up their home in the dower house at Luttons Park. Clara had been a close friend of Sarah's and, while in those days Sarah had sometimes dreamed of being wed to Philip herself, she had been pleased to see Clara and Philip so happy together. A year later, Clara had died giving birth to a stillborn daughter, and Philip had been inconsolable. Fortunately, he still had the estate to occupy him and he and Sarah had remained good friends.

Now, she returned to the subject of Bertram's wooing. 'I cannot marry Bertram even for Mama's sake. I do not love him,' she said to Philip, who put out a hand to her and touched her cheek.

'And what do you know of love, my goose?' he teased her.

'You may mock me if you like for I know I am at my last prayers at four-and-twenty, but I do know that I have no feelings of love for Bertram though I do hold him in great respect . . . oh, Philip, I am forgetting my news. You will never guess what has happened, I must hurry home and tell Mama.'

'You cannot go without telling me first,' he chided.

Sarah told him of the visit of Julian Cleeve and he listened attentively.

'Don't go falling in love with him, Sarah, he might whisk you back to America.'

'No, no,' she was quick to say. 'It is his intention to settle at Cleeve Grange and his daughter is only a little younger than Marianne. I cannot wait to tell her.'

Philip leapt on his horse. 'Off you go and do not forget to tell Bertram that he has an American rival.'

Sarah laughed. 'You are impossible,' she said and watched him ride off to Luttons Park. Dear Philip, she thought, I wonder if anyone will ever come along who will be to him as Clara was. He deserves better than to remain a bachelor for the rest of his life. And she gave a chuckle. I do not suppose I would be hesitating if it was Philip who was asking for my hand and not Bertram.

She walked on and let herself in the front door of Little Cleeve not knowing what to expect as her mother had been seen off from Cleeve Grange verging on a fit of the vapours, indeed almost hysterical.

Lady Hadlow's eldest daughter was greeted in the small entrance hall by a stocky country gentleman of neat dress, a florid complexion and, at that moment, an air of vexation.

'Sarah, where have you been all this time? You must have known that your mother needed you. I've had the devil's own job – I beg your pardon for my language, you can tell that I am at a pass – it has been very difficult to make Lady Hadlow a little more composed. She will not stop crying unless I sit and hold her hand.'

Sarah found herself without words for a moment. Standing in front of her and rather stiffly, was the portly figure of Sir Bertram Hesslewood. He had promised to visit them that morning to help them in their removal to Little Cleeve, but Sarah knew that the visit would occasion yet another offer of marriage.

For of late, Sir Bertram had decided that he must have an heir and that the Hon. Sarah Winterson would make a suitable wife and mother to his children. Every time they met, he would renew his offer and totally ignore her protestations and refusal of his suit.

Sarah had never enjoyed the benefits of a season, for her father had been ill and had then died penniless when she should have been making her come-out. So, no offers had come her way and she had considered herself on the shelf when along had come Sir Bertram and asked for her hand in marriage.

As Philip had said, Sir Bertram was almost the same age as Sarah's mother and, when he had made his declaration, Lady Hadlow had been delighted and Sarah appalled. She had known him for ever to be a conceited bore of a man, wealthy enough and generous to his brother, but puffed up with his own importance at being the most substantial landowner in Bidborough, terming himself the squire.

'Well, Sarah, you seem to have gone into a daze. Do not tell me that you are overturned as well; I credit you with more sense.'

Sarah looked at the man who wished to marry her and not for

the first time found that neither his features nor his expression gave her any confidence let alone joy. He was not a tall man but well-built and accustomed to an outdoor life. He followed the hounds keenly and spent many hours in the saddle around his vast estate, so well managed by his younger brother.

He had dignity, she had to admit, and he was a kind man, but she did not love him and would not consider his offer, though there were times when she wondered if she should marry him for the sake and welfare of her mother and Marianne and James.

At that moment, she felt an irritation with him and found to her horror that her voice was sharp. Sir Bertram had been kind in his attention to her mother that morning, but Sarah found it irksome to have him in the house when she needed to speak urgently to Lady Hadlow about financial matters. Also to tell her of their cousin's arrival on the scene.

'I am sorry, Bertram, I find myself distracted, this morning. I cannot tell you why until I have spoken to Mama. It was kind of you to come and bear with her nervous humours. I appreciate your kindness and thoughtfulness very much, but I must decline to offer you a nuncheon as it is imperative that I speak to Mama on her own.'

Sir Bertram was a good-natured man and did not take offence easily. So he made a slight bow and took Sarah's hand. Sarah felt the limpness of his touch and was immediately jolted into the remembrance of the stronger grasp she had received that morning from her cousin.

Sir Bertram spoke seriously. 'Something has occurred to disturb you, Sarah, I can tell. Would you not rather confide in me and not worry your poor mother who is already overset with her nerves?'

'Thank you Bertram, it is kind of you. But Mama must know that our cousin Julian Cleeve has arrived in this country and is staying in Tunbridge Wells.'

'He has had the audacity to call on the day he has turned you out of your home?'

'He was not to know that we were on the move today, Bertram.'

'I suppose not.' He pressed her hand and walked to the door. 'I will leave you to break the news to your poor mama; he is of her family, after all.'

'But, Bertram, I must tell you. . . .'

'No, go and tend to your mama, I think she is in need of your firm hand. Marianne is much too gentle with her. Good morning.'

'Good morning, Bertram.'

Sarah sighed as she heard him walk round to the stables. I did not tell him that Mama's cousin had died and that it is his son who is here, she thought. And a son who is young and handsome and who I am sure can be no more than thirty-six years of age even if he does have a daughter of eighteen. And for the first time that day, at the thought of Julian Cleeve and Sir Bertram Hesslewood together, she felt her sense of humour return to her.

Two

AS SOON AS Sarah saw her mother, she knew that it would be impossible to talk about financial matters with the stricken woman.

The drawing-room at Little Cleeve was both spacious and comfortable, there was no denying it. The windows were small and the ceiling low, but there was a handsome marble fireplace in which a fire burned cheerfully; the furniture and the carpet were in excellent taste. The house had been unused for over four years, but the maids from the Grange had kept the rooms both clean and well-aired.

But the scene before Sarah was neither bright nor comforting. Her mother lay on a *chaise-longue* and Sarah could hear her sobs. Her sister Marianne sat by her side and was holding her mother's hand, at the same time clutching a vinaigrette which seemed to serve no purpose at all.

Marianne was as different from Sarah as it was possible for two sisters to be; the one tall and dark, with hair that would not curl except with the use of rags or papers, and the younger girl presenting a competely different picture. Marianne was short and small-boned, and gave a dainty if somewhat fragile appearance; her mouth, nose and chin were well shaped and neat in a heart-shaped face. Her eyes were blue and her hair hung loose in gold ringlets. In short, she was a very pretty girl, but she was not concerned about her looks, being modest in her behaviour and caring in her manner.

When she saw Sarah come into the room, she got up and ran towards her, throwing her arms round the taller girl. 'Sarah, thank goodness you have come. What has detained you for so long? I have not known what to do with Mama. She will not stop crying and you would think it was the end of the world when here we are, nice and warm and cosy. It was Bertram who saved the day, I must tell you. He held Mama's hand and talked soothingly to her, very firmly, too. I must admire him and I do not as a rule for I always thought it was ridiculous of him to make an offer for you. In the end, he had to go; you must have met him on your way in, I am sure. As soon as he was out of the door, Mama started to cry again.'

Sarah listened to the tale then hastened to her mother's side. Lady Hadlow stopped crying when she saw her eldest daughter and held out her hand. It became quite obvious when one saw her that it was from her mother that Marianne had inherited her pretty looks. Lady Hadlow presented a frail but pleasing appearance; she was small and slim and her hair still held the gold of her youth. She had been married when only eighteen and had presented Lord Hadlow with Sarah a year later; so that now, although Sarah felt old-maidish at four-and-twenty, Lady Hadlow was little more than forty years of age. She had been dominated all her life by the forcefulness of Lord Hadlow's personality, and left without him and with no money, she had declined into a poor creature.

'Sarah, what has kept you? I felt the need of you but I must tell you that dear Bertram has been kindness itself. He has only just this minute left us and has been the source of much comfort to me. He has even been holding my hand all the morning.'

Sarah felt an unexpected rush of laughter within her as the thought came to her, and just as Philip had suggested, that perhaps

Bertram would do better for her mother than for herself.

But she turned to Lady Hadlow and was quite serious. 'Mama, you can stop your tears for I have some good news for you. Not only that, when I was walking down the drive from the Grange, it struck me that Little Cleeve is such an elegant house even if it is smaller than we are used to. And here you are in this very pleasant room and I am sure that we will go along quite well.'

Lady Hadlow sighed. 'Perhaps you are right, dear, for I find it much more spacious than I remembered it to be. But what news can you possibly have received in the space of a morning since we left Cleeve Grange?'

Sarah smiled. 'We had a visitor.'

'A visitor? What do you mean?'

'I was not best pleased at first for I thought it to be a most inconvenient time to call. But I soon learned that it was none other than our Cousin Julian from America . . . yes, you may look amazed for I know it is he who has turned us out. But this is a young man; your cousin died a year ago, then his son was widowed and he wishes to make his home in England. He has come over here with his young daughter, Anita, who is only a year younger than Marianne.' Sarah heard her sister give a little gasp and she turned and smiled at the younger girl.

'Yes, Marianne, I do think that Anita would be a companion for you and, as her father intends to give her a season in Tunbridge Wells, I see no reason why you should not join her. I have not spoken about it to Cousin Julian yet as I hardly know him, but we will see what can be done.'

Marianne was all smiles for a few seconds, but then her expression changed. 'It is kind of you to think of me, Sarah, but you know as well as I do that our finances do not allow for fine clothes. Not that I wish to be especially stylish all the time, but attending the assemblies in Tunbridge Wells would mean that I should need several gowns and nice dresses.'

Sarah looked from her sister to her mother who, she was pleased to see, had forgotten her tears. But still she felt that she could not mention the debt to their American cousin and spoke cheerfully. 'I cannot promise anything, Marianne, but we will see what we can do, won't we, Mama?'

Lady Hadlow raised herself from the cushions. 'If we have sacrificed our home at Cleeve Grange in order to give Marianne a season, then it will all be worth while. She is such a pretty little thing, even if I say it myself, and I am sure she would obtain a good offer.' But she was looking at Sarah and not at Marianne. 'Sarah, do you not think that Sir Bertram would provide for a season for Marianne?'

The pointed question vexed Sarah more than she would have thought possible and her reply was short and sharp. 'I am not prepared to ask Bertram for any such thing. Please do not mention it again. We will come about somehow.'

'Very well, Sarah,' replied her mother, reclining gracefully on the *chaise-longue*, her attitude of woe rapidly changing to one of high expectations that perhaps the arrival of her cousin's wealthy son would prove to be to their advantage.

In all the years since Lord Hadlow's death and his squandering of what little fortune he had at the gaming table, Sarah had insisted that they kept their small carriage. Her mother visited in the area and then there were trips into Tunbridge Wells. They had only three horses in the stables; Spark – who was quite the opposite of his name – for the carriage, Turk, who was James's beloved hunter and was kept exercised for their brother by the faithful Reuben, and Cilla, Sarah's very own and reliable mare.

So the following morning, after a restless night dreaming she was still at the Grange but married to Philip Hesslewood, Sarah was glad to dress in her one decent morning gown. It was of a deep green cotton, high to the neck and with long sleeves which were tight at the wrists. With it she wore a spencer of a soft, paler shade of green and she knew she looked well for a business trip into Tunbridge Wells.

Reuben had moved from the Grange with them and was installed in the tiny cottage attached to the stables. Sarah ordered the carriage and he did not take long to have it at the gate of Little Cleeve and was waiting cheerfully to drive her into the town.

In spite of being beset with worry as to how they could possibly pay the rent owing to their cousin, Sarah felt unusually optimistic. Lady Hadlow had recovered from her fit of the megrims and had eaten a good breakfast in their new dining-room, there being no breakfast-room at Little Cleeve. Marianne had woken with a bright face at the prospect of having a cousin of her own age as her neighbour even though she was aware that her wardrobe was woefully inadequate.

Sarah had grown up with Tunbridge Wells as her nearest town, but had been denied any of the advantages the fashionable watering-place had to offer. The small town had been all the rage in the previous century under the auspices of Beau Nash, and if the Regent had found it dull and preferred to make Brighton his own, the Assembly Rooms and the Theatre had been built and it remained a lively and pleasant town.

Sarah made her way along the Parade to the lawyer's office; she walked under the colonnade on the paving of Purbeck stone which had replaced the original pantiles; she passed coffee houses and taverns, milliners and drapers. Tunbridge Wells had everything to offer that the visitor needed including the Chalybeate Spring where it was possible to drink the health-giving waters.

Mr Lumley's office was towards the end of the Parade near the Swan Hotel; the small building was also his home and he had his office on the ground floor.

Sarah was used to doing business with him and did not feel ill-at-ease as many young ladies of four-and-twenty might have done at entering his office. His clerk received her and a few minutes later, she was sitting facing the now elderly Mr Lumley across his wide desk.

Although in his sixties, Josiah Lumley looked younger for he had lived a sober life and was a respected citizen of Tunbridge Wells. Only his white hair betrayed his age as he got up, shook Sarah by the hand and drew up a chair for her.

'My dear Miss Winterson, I trust that all has gone well with your move to Little Cleeve? I am afraid that your mama will not have taken the change easily.'

Sarah smiled. She could speak honestly to Mr Lumley, for there was nothing he did not know about the family. 'She was most agitated, I fear, but she seems more cheerful this morning. Little Cleeve is smaller than we are used to, but I am sure we will soon be at home there.' Then she remembered the purpose of her visit. 'But, Mr Lumley, I received some disturbing news yesterday and have come to ask your advice.'

'I hope it is nothing I cannot put right for you, Miss Winterson.'

'I hope so, too,' said Sarah and proceeded to tell him of Julian Cleeve's visit and the outcome of their conversation.

Mr Lumley's expression changed as Sarah spoke. He showed a genuine interest that the American cousin had arrived, regret that old Mr Cleeve had died and then a concern which bordered on horror when Sarah told him about the rents.

'Miss Winterson,' he interrupted her. 'I am appalled. It was all settled at the time of Lord Hadlow's death. Let me find the papers.' He got up and searched through a large cabinet, coming back to his desk with a sheaf of papers which he proceeded to glance through.

'Yes, yes,' he nodded. 'I thought so.' He turned to her. 'It is as I thought, Miss Winterson. Now I may have to say things that are painful to you. but you must know the whole. You are aware that in the years before he died, Lord Hadlow was much addicted to gaming and that long before his decease, his funds had run dangerously low. He came to see me and told me that he had written to his American cousin and asked to be excused the rent for a year of so. Then he said that a reply had come from Mr Cleeve saying that as Cleeve Grange had been cared for all those years and he had no intention of returning to England, he would gladly waive any more payments.' The lawyer lookd at Sarah across the top of his spectacles.

'He did not show me the letter, but he gave me the instruction to send no more rents. I made a note of it and I have it here. No money has been paid since that day. My dear, Miss Winterson, I hardly know what to say. Your father told me to send no more money, your cousin's father has said that money was owing to him. What would you wish me to do?'

Sarah shook her head. 'It is very difficult. I think the best thing would be for me to have another talk with my cousin.' She paused. 'Mr Lumley, can you tell me what the sum would be? The amount that is owing, I mean.'

Mr Lumley dipped his pen in the standish and scribbled some figures on a sheet of paper, murmuring as he did so. 'The rent was ludicrously low, almost laughable in fact, but the fact remains that your father was in such straits that he could not pay. You well know of the difficulties we have had in paying off his gaming debts and to keep any knowledge from your poor mother. There, just over four years; the total sum would be about two hundred pounds, perhaps a little more.'

Sarah looked dismayed. 'We do not have that much, do we, Mr Lumley?'

'I am afraid not,' he replied. 'With the expense of sending young Lord Hadlow to Oxford, there is only enough left for your everyday needs.' He frowned a little. 'One thing does puzzle me, and that is the letter I received from America telling me of your cousin wishing to live at Cleeve Grange. It gave no indication that it was from the younger Mr Cleeve or that his father had died. Indeed, it was the briefest of notes and quite peremptory.'

Sarah was thinking of her encounter of the previous morning and she spoke slowly. 'Mr Cleeve seemed very guarded to begin with yesterday morning, but once he had told me about his father's death and how he planned to live at Cleeve Grange with his young daughter – he is a widower, by the way – then I thought he became more open. I had the impression that it was most important to him to make a new life in England.'

'Would you like me to see Mr Cleeve for you, Miss Winterson?'

Sarah was thoughtful. 'It is kind of you to offer but I think I would like to approach him myself. I expect him and his daughter at Little Cleeve in a day or so and that will give me the opportunity to speak to him about it all.' She looked at the kindly lawyer and gave a smile. 'I can always pass him on to you if he is difficult?'

'You have courage, Miss Winterson and I admire you for it. It is not an easy time for you.'

She left Mr Lumley and carried out a few commissions in the town, including a visit to the Fish Market; then Reuben took her back to Little Cleeve where she told her mother nothing of her visit to the lawyer and produced the fresh fish as the purpose of her visit before handing it over to the capable Ellen.

Later that afternoon, the payment of the arrears of the rent still uppermost in her mind, Sarah knew that the only person she could trust with her problem was Philip. For as long as she could remember, she had been able to turn to him and he had been her mainstay in the difficult years following her father's death.

She often wondered about her feelings for Philip and the regard they had for one another; their closeness at times of trouble, their shared confidences, their experiences in the care of their own countryside, their ability to laugh at things together. It is like a litany, she would say to herself, but does it amount to what could be a lasting love?

Philip declares himself a bachelor, she would argue, even though he is widowed, but he has the Luttons dower house as his home and seems comfortable. She felt it would be enough for her – she did not crave riches except for her family – and thought that she could be happy with him; his quiet nature nicely balanced her more tempestuous one.

But she put her idle thoughts on one side and enjoyed a gallop on Cilla towards Luttons. As she arrived at Luttons Park, she wondered whether to seek out Philip at the big house or at his home.

Luttons Park itself was an imposing country mansion built in parkland a hundred years earlier. In character, it was not unlike Cleeve Grange, but to Sarah, it seemed to lack the grace which gave the Grange its distinctiveness. In contrast, because of its grand setting, Luttons appeared formal, even unfriendly.

Sarah looked at the house and then thought of Bertram. Her heart sank. I just cannot imagine being mistress of Luttons Park, it does not feel like *me*. I think Mama would love it, but how can I persuade Bertram that Mama would suit him best? And she laughed quietly; it is an heir Bertram needs and Mama could hardly oblige him at her age. What wicked thoughts, she said to herself, I must try and find Philip.

Just as she was about to head Cilla in the direction of the dower house, she spotted a figure riding round from the stables behind Luttons Park and saw to her relief that it was Philip. I am in luck after all, she decided and rode up towards him.

'Hallo, little one,' was Philip's greeting. 'Were you looking for me or my big brother?'

'I am trying to avoid your big brother,' she replied. 'And it is twenty years since I was your little one, Philip Hesslewood, I am grown up now.'

'I know, Sarah, but I still love to tease you just as I did then. There is a kind of timelessness in it which I rather like . . . but do I see a little frown of worry in your eyes?'

'Yes, Philip; do you mind if I bring my troubles to you?' she asked him.

'Who else could you take them to? Come along, let us ride down to the lake and we can sit and watch the ducks. Do you remember I used to get into trouble for throwing stones at them?'

Sarah managed a smile. 'You were a wicked little boy. I think you only did it to make your sisters cross.'

'You loved me then, did you not?' he said.

'It was hero-worship,' she said. 'You could do no wrong in my eyes . . . and then you met Clara.'

They were silent, back in a past which shared happy childhood memories with all the worries and sadness of their later years.

'Out with it, Sarah, what is the new worry? Is it the American cousin or is it Bertram?'

'It is neither, it is a legacy of my father.'

'You are never still suffering from Lord Hadlow's excesses, are you? Tell me.'

And Sarah did tell him. The two of them sat on the stone steps at the foot of a statue which ornamented the lakeside. It was a place of many such discussions.

Philip's arm came round her shoulders as she finished her explanation and she was content to leave it there and to feel the comfort and reassurance it gave her.

'I can understand you wanting to put the matter right, Sarah, but from what you have told me of your cousin, I think it is a very little sum to him.'

'But I do not want to be indebted to him.'

'You did not like him?' he asked.

'Not at first, yet I think he could be a caring sort of person.' And she told him about Mrs Lingfield and he nodded.

'I can think of only two ways out of the trouble, Sarah.'

She looked at him and saw that he was serious. 'You mean that I should marry Bertram, do you not?'

'Yes: he would not notice the payment of the arrears for it would be a paltry sum to him.'

Sarah did not speak for a moment. 'I suppose it is too much to hope that I should marry someone whom I could love,' was all she said. 'What was the other thing, Philip?'

'That you let me pay it,' he said quietly.

But this did not suit Sarah either. 'Philip, you are a younger son, though I know you have the dower house and Bertram pays you a good salary for running the estate for him. I know I rarely speak of Clara, but you will want to have your own family one day and she would not have expected you to live the life of a recluse . . . I am sorry if I say things that hurt, Philip.'

'You would never hurt me, Sarah, and I am not a recluse as long as we can carry our troubles to each other. I appreciate that and I am content to let it be. If ever I meet someone I can love as I loved Clara, then I would marry again, but I will not give my heart lightly.' He tried to force a cheerfulness into their conversation. 'Now how about this debt of yours, you will permit me to pay it?'

'Thank you, Philip, I do appreciate your offer, but I would simply be exchanging one debtor for another. I think I will have another word with my cousin and see if we cannot come to some arrangement. He was willing to wipe off the debt, but I will not have it that way. It took me years to settle all Papa's gaming debts and I will not let myself get into the same position again. You do understand, Philip?'

He got to his feet and pulled her from the steps. 'I do understand and all I will say is that you know where to find me. Now let us throw off the blues and I will race you back to Little Cleeve.'

She gave a short laugh of delight for they had had this race on horseback so many times and she always lost.

'You never let me win,' she told him.

'I should think not,' he replied instantly and with a smile.

*

Less than two days were to pass before a curricle pulled up outside Little Cleeve and the two Winterson girls rushed to the window in time to see the tall gentleman who was their cousin handing down a young lady who looked older than Sarah had imagined.

'Cousin Julian,' said Sarah. 'And that must be Anita; she looks older than her years.'

The visitors were admitted by Nancy their willing servant who acted as parlour-maid, serving-maid and housemaid as well as being a great help to Lady Hadlow with her toilette. She showed them into the drawing-room and Sarah hurried to greet them.

'Cousin Julian,' she said, and hoped that she sounded welcoming. 'And this is Anita.'

She shook hands and bent to kiss the girl at his side who looked younger as she stood beside her father. They soon discovered that she was eighteen years of age and only a year behind Marianne. Dressed in a stylish dark-red pelisse with matching bonnet, her face beneath it was pale but not plain. She had the same bright blue eyes as Marianne and her small features were appealing; in some way, it was the expression in her eyes which made her look older.

Sarah was thinking all this as she spoke to them. 'Come and meet my mother.'

Lady Hadlow had got up from the *chaise-longue* and, her hand in her cousin's, he bent over it with a nice courtesy and Sarah was pleased to see that her mother was smiling.

'Mama, this is your Cousin Julian and his daughter, Anita. Cousin Julian, Lady Hadlow. And this is my younger sister, Marianne.' She stopped and gave a laugh. 'Oh, what a lot of introductions. I am sure we will get to know one another very shortly. Please sit down.'

Julian Cleeve was still holding on to Lady Hadlow's hand and was speaking pleasantly to her. 'I hope you are not regarding me as an ogre who has turned you out of your home, Cousin. And we really are cousins in a remote way. I believe I have it right. Your brother's wife took her Cousin Margaret with her to Virginia and Margaret met and married Julian Cleeve and she was, of course, my mother. As you know, your brother died and I had no cousins in America; my Aunt Joan married again and moved away so I am afraid we lost touch. You are my only surviving relatives and it gives me great pleasure to be able to meet you.'

Sarah was entertaining wicked thoughts. He is nothing but a charmer, she was saying to herself; first Mrs Lingfield and now the look on Mama's face is nothing short of doting. We will have to see if he is as charming when I do battle with him about the rents.

She turned to see that Anita had taken off her pelisse and bonnet and was in animated conversation with Marianne. Although the two girls were the same in age, height and build, there the resemblance ended. Anita was as dark as Marianne was fair, and her hair was straight and swept up rather than dropping in the fashionable ringlets; they shared only the same blue of their eyes.

Sarah could see that Julian Cleeve was regarding the pair with a pleased expression on his face. He turned to Sarah with a smile.

'I think the two of them are made for each other, Sarah, and I am so pleased to find someone of Anita's age here at Little Cleeve.'

Sarah knew that the moment had come to speak of the vexed questions of debts. 'It will be nice for Marianne, too, there are very few girls of her age in the neighbourhood. But Cousin Julian—'

'Julian, please.'

She gave a short laugh. 'Julian, I have to talk to you on a business matter and I do not wish my mother to hear our conversation. Would you care to walk in the garden with me?'

'Yes, of course. I have a lot of things about which I need to seek your advice.'

'I would not have thought that you were the kind of person who would accept advice easily,' she replied quickly, the words seeming to slip from her of their own free will. There was something in her cousin which made her feel a lack of respect and she was at a loss to understand it. She would never have spoken to either Bertram or Philip in such a way.

But he only gave a short chuckle. 'You will find me most agreeable except when I am thwarted about anything,' he said, and she sensed with relief that he was teasing her.

'I can believe it and I must be careful of what I say to you!' Julian Cleeve looked at the girl who was bearing so much on her young shoulders. He had seen at a glance that Lady Hadlow was of an invalidish nature and would be of little use; also that the pretty little Marianne needed to be better dressed and given a chance to enter into society. But looking at Sarah, he saw a girl who was not quite beautiful but whose handsome good looks betrayed a will of iron and probably a streak of obstinacy.

Then he glanced around him. Lady Hadlow was reclining on her cushions once again and Anita and Marianne were still chattering and laughing happily together. The sight of the two of them gave him an idea, but he was careful to keep it at the back of his mind.

'Shall we go into the garden then, Sarah? You have gardens at the back of Little Cleeve? There is little at the front, I noticed.'

She nodded. 'Yes, come out of the front door and we will walk round by the stables. I am afraid I had to bring Reuben with us, he has been our right hand as long as I remember. Have you succeeded in getting a coachman? I see that you are driving your curricle, but I expect you will need a carriage.'

'Sir Roger has been most helpful to me. They live in a big house on the London Road and, as Lady Elizabeth says, they rattle around now that their children are married and have left home. There is only the youngest daughter at home now; Jane, as I think I told you, and I believe that Lady Elizabeth was pleased to have Anita in the house as a companion for her. There is an open invitation for Anita to visit them and I am hoping that Jane will come over to Cleeve Grange. She is younger than Anita, but at that age it does not seem to matter as long as they have a fashion book to pore over.' He glanced down at her. 'But that is not what I was meaning to tell you. Sir Roger has supplied me with a good man from his own stables and I have purchased a carriage which he will bring tomorrow.'

They stepped into the back garden and Sarah apologized. 'It is no more than a shrubbery, I am afraid, but Reuben has kept the bushes clipped all these years. I think you will find it rather small.'

Julian found himself looking down a winding path through groups of shrubs; some clipped and dark green, others showing the first flowers of the spring. There were trees he did not know and the end of the garden was marked by a box hedge and then the small copse and wood-walk which gave a sheltered feel to the small haven of green.

'I like it,' he said. 'So let us stroll through the shrubs and trees, most of which are strangers to me. You must not forget that I have come from tobacco acres which, to say the least of it, are monotonous. This is very English and very pleasant. Now you must tell me what is worrying you and what it was you could not say in front of your mama.'

Sarah stopped. She wanted to face him and could not do so as long as they were walking through the garden.

'I have been to see our lawyer and have uncovered a strange state of affairs. I know now that we are in debt to you for the sum of about two hundred pounds and I am determined to repay it though I do not know how at the moment. . . .'

'My dear Sarah—'

'I am not your dear Sarah, our acquaintance is only two days old and I wish to be businesslike.'

'Very well. Tell me what else the lawyer said.'

'He told me that he had sent no rent on instructions from your father. I have to tell you that my father was a profligate and a gamester and, before he died, our finances were at a standstill. He wrote to our Cousin Julian ~ your father, that is – and asked if the rent could be deferred for a year or two until he came about. He received a reply telling him that because he had taken care of the property, the rents would be waived. Then he gave an instruction to Mr Lumley, our lawyer, not to send any more money and that is why you have received nothing.'

Sarah was now facing Julian Cleeve and their eyes met; hers perplexed, his expressionless. 'Then why did my father complain that no rent had been paid?' he asked her. 'Did you see the letters?'

'No, neither did Mr Lumley. He simply wrote down Papa's instruction and then followed it . . .' she faltered. 'You think Papa was making it all up in order to avoid having to find the money?' she asked miserably.

His hands went out and grasped her arms; she could feel the warmth of his fingers through the cotton sleeve. 'I don't know, Sarah, I just don't know. We will wipe off the debt. Our fathers are both of them dead and we can never know the truth. It is best forgotten. Two hundred pounds is nothing to me; you must have realized that I am a man of considerable fortune. Some of it I have worked for, some of it I have inherited, and now I have Cleeve Grange, as well. We must forget a paltry debt like that. Let us shake hands on it.'

In reply, Sarah pulled her arms from his grasp and lost her temper at the same time. 'Two hundred pounds may be nothing to you, but it is a fortune to us. And I will not be in debt, do you hear?' She knew she was shouting at him but she did not care. 'I have spent a lifetime trying to bear with my father's debts and the last four years attempting to clear them. I have almost succeeded and you arrive on the scene and we discover that we owe two hundrd pounds. I cannot forget it and I will pay every penny of it. If we have to eat fish and potatoes for a year, I will repay the money, do you understand?'

To her shame and horror, Sarah found that she was stamping her foot and that tears of anger were trickling down her cheeks. She dashed them away with a hand and turned from him while she calmed herself.

'Sarah,' came a soft voice that did not sound as though it belonged to him at all. She half-turned towards him. 'I am sorry that my remark made you cry. Let me wipe your tears away.'

Sarah was instantly on her guard. 'I do not wish for your sympathy. I am sure you are being kind only because I lost my temper and shouted at you. I will pay back the money somehow, Cousin Julian.'

'Julian.'

'Very well then, I will forget the cousin. You are abominable.'

'So you said when we first met,' he reminded her.

'It was only two days ago,' she retorted.

'Yes, I know. I have a feeling that it was a good day when I came to Cleeve Grange.' He took her by the hand and started walking slowly towards the wood walk where he had seen a rustic bench. 'Look, Sarah, let us sit and allow me to tell you of an idea that has come to me. In fact, I thought of it earlier, but did not know I would have need of it so soon.'

'What do you mean? Have you thought of something cheaper than fish and potatoes?' Sarah was aghast. She knew herself to be spirited, but she was not usually tempted into impertinence. Yet there seemed to be some unknown quantity in her cousin which gave her permission to be free with her words.

'I will ignore that remark, Sarah. Sit down with me and listen.'

Three

SARAH SAT STILL on the rough bench at the end of the garden looking back towards the house. She still thought that Little Cleeve had a charm and proportion of its own; perhaps it lies in the mellowed stone, she said to herself.

In front of her, a new home, and beside her, an elegant stranger who seemed to be able to surprise or annoy her at every turn of phrase. She wondered what he could possibly have to suggest that would alleviate the problem of having to find the £200 to pay their debt.

'Are you listening to me, Sarah?' His voice came through her thoughts.

'Yes, of course.'

'Anita and I have settled into Cleeve Grange with the excellent Mrs Lingfield, and we shall soon have Mrs Stockdale as our housekeeper. Lady Elizabeth has procured her services and she is coming in the carriage in the morning together with my new coachman. So I have made a lot of progress in very little time and I am feeling pleased. But there is one big problem remaining – I should say that there are two problems, but it is the first one which occupies my mind the most and I would like to tell you about it; the second, I will ask for your good advice.'

'I might give my advice but I doubt you would take it,' she returned swiftly.

'Be quiet.'

'Very well.' Sarah was not used to talking to a gentleman in this vein. It puzzled her.

Her cousin continued. 'It is of the first importance to me that I find a companion for Anita; she cannot be at Cleeve Grange on her own while I am out and around the estate as I hope to be. I do not wish for an older person because I think that young company would draw Anita out of her diffidence and shyness because of her limp. If we are in Tunbridge Wells, she has Jane Humphries, but I need someone here at Cleeve Grange. You can guess my thoughts?'

Sarah's reply was genuine. 'No, I cannot.' And she really meant it for she had only seen an Anita who had been on instantly friendly terms with Marianne and certainly showing no signs of shyness or diffidence.

'As we were leaving Little Cleeve just now,' he continued, 'I could not but help notice that Anita and Marianne seemed to be getting along very well together and the thought came to me then that perhaps Marianne would make the companion I need for Anita. They are almost the same age and have the same interests . . . no, don't interrupt. . . .' His tone was serious.

'I want to get to the bottom of this business of the wretched rent. I would expect to pay Anita's companion a salary – and it would be a generous one to the right person – but I suggest that we ask Marianne to come along without being paid anything. Then I would be in your debt and it would all cancel out. What do you think?'

Sarah sat in silence. It made sense and it would be a splendid opportunity for Marianne but . . . her thoughts burst out into words. 'I do not want to be beholden to you for anything,' she said grudgingly.

'Now come along, you would not be beholden to me, it would

be the other way round. I would be in debt to you for providing us with Marianne and. . . .' he broke off and looked at her keenly. 'Confess that you would like it for Marianne's sake.'

She gave in. 'Yes, that is true. In fact, it would be Marianne who would be the financial sufferer for she could go as a paid companion any one of these days. But Mama would never allow it. The daughter of Lady Hadlow a paid companion? Never! I think she would rather just live on potatoes.'

'And no fish.'

They both laughed and then discussed the plan eagerly.

'And you will not mind if I take Marianne to stay with the Humphries in Tunbridge Wells from time to time?'

But there Sarah faltered. 'But Marianne knows that she has neither suitable dresses nor gowns to wear in society.'

Julian did not hesitate. 'Do not worry for a minute about that. I will provide her with whatever she needs.'

Sarah instantly flared. 'But then I would be in your debt again.'

He turned and took her by the shoulders. 'You wretched girl, are you never satisfied? Shall I demand payment in a kiss?'

Sarah got up from the bench hastily. 'No, you will not; how dare you. Do all American gentlemen behave in this way?'

'There are no gentlemen in America. We are all settlers, though Father did his best to educate me into the ways of English society. Do you think he succeeded?'

Their eyes clashed. 'I am not sure. You are not like other gentlemen I know. There is a rakishness about you.'

'Is that bad?' he taunted.

'Very bad.'

He laughed aloud. 'I like that. The rakish American, that is what I will be. But I can tell you one thing, my dear cousin, I shall only ask for kisses from you, no one else.'

'And you will not get them from me.' She answered him stubbornly and with another flare of temper.

'We will see. Now we must talk about Marianne and Anita again. Are we agreed that your pretty sister will become Anita's companion and that if we go to the assemblies – I think you call them – in Tunbridge Wells, then I shall have the dressing of both girls? It will give me a good deal of pleasure, Sarah. I've had a grim year and it is time I started to enjoy myself and my fortune. Anita, too.'

'Cousin Julian . . . I am sorry, Julian, you are really very kind, are you not? You put on this austere and elegant appearance and haughty expression yet underneath, I do believe you have a kindness in you.'

'You do not know me, Sarah, and you might yet change your mind.'

She thought it a strange remark and could not begin to work it out so she asked him another question.

'Why did you say that you wanted to ask my advice?'

He smiled. 'You can tell me about my steward or whoever has had the excellent running of the Cleeve estate: it all seems to be in very good order.'

'I am glad you think so,' Sarah said.

'Will you kindly tell me his name and if he is likely to continue with me?'

'It is not a "he".'

He stared at her but could only see laughter in her eyes, although her expression was serious.

'What nonsense are you talking?'

'The steward is a "she",' Sarah told him.

'A woman? You mean that in this country you have women as stewards? I don't believe it.'

'No, you need not believe it for it is most unusual.'

'You are talking in riddles. Who has been the steward of Cleeve Grange?'

'I have.'

Julian Cleeve, with his haughty look, stood up then and towered over her. 'You infuriating girl. I am being serious and I would be grateful if you could be serious with me. Now let us start again. Who has been steward at Cleeve Grange all these years?'

Sarah looked up at him this time, her eyes dancing with fun. 'I have,' she repeated. 'And for heaven's sake, sit down and I will tell you about it if you wish to know.'

He did sit down. He sat close and took her hand in his. 'Of course I wish to know. I have a feeling that you are not playing with me and I demand to know the truth of the matter. Please tell me your tale, my sweet.'

'I am not your—'

'My sweet? No, I do not think you are sweet, you are much too independent-minded to be called sweet, and I like it. I ask you again to tell me your tale.'

'Be prepared for a long one, but I will give you permission to interrupt if you wish.'

'Thank you,' he said drily.

Sarah sat silently for a moment; she was back in the past and Julian sensed this.

'How many years, Sarah?'

She looked up at him and gave a grin for she knew exactly what he was meaning. 'About twenty years, just about as long as I can remember, I suppose. My father had a steward named Toby Rochester; he was a jolly fellow but somewhat idle. He was not regular in collecting the rents from the farms and not good at listening to the tenants' problems. They did not like him. I do not suppose I ever knew what kind of wage he was paid, but he was a bachelor and lived at Little Cleeve on his own, rent free.'

'Did he take care of the house?'

'No, he was most neglectful, but that is another story. The next thing I can remember was that he was dressing himself in a stylish manner and going off to gaming establishments with my father. I can't blame Toby for I believe that Papa led him into it.' She turned to him. 'Am I taking too long?'

'No, may I hold your hand?'

'Why do you ask? Are you suddenly polite?'

'You are a shrew!'

'Here is a shrew's hand then.' And Sarah held out her hand to him and thought she must be going mad. But she let her hand lie in his and continued her story.

'That all seemed to go on for a long time – until my father died, in fact. That was nearly four years ago and by then he was in Dun Territory. My mother was useless, Marianne was still very young and James was away at school. I was twenty years of age, my affections were not engaged, so I took it upon myself to put things right. After all, we still had a house if nothing else.'

'I am glad of that.' He made the comment quietly.

She looked at him. 'You really mean that, do you not?'

'Yes, I do. Continue.'

Sarah obeyed him without changing her expression. 'The first thing I did was to get rid of Toby, shut up Little Cleeve and take on the estate myself. I had often ridden out to collect the rents and I had always got on well with the farmers and their wives. I think our neighbours were scandalized, but they soon got used to me doing the rounds of the estate on horseback or in the pony-cart. I suppose you will probably think it unnatural in a young lady, but I enjoyed myself.'

'I admire you, Sarah.'

'Thank you very much.' She looked to see if he was serious and his eyes told her that he was. 'We gradually pulled through; Mr Lumley was a great help to me. We paid off Papa's gaming debts and we even managed to send James to Oxford. I did not have a season but I did not mind that. I cared more that Marianne should have one, but I could not imagine how we could achieve it.'

'And you did not starve?'

She laughed. 'No, the farmers' wives were most generous for they all knew our situation. Never a week would go by that they did not send us a fowl or a saddle of mutton.'

'And what about your clothes?'

'I needed very little and Marianne is a very clever needle-woman and can make most of her dresses or alter them from mine or Mama's. She also made all the hangings for Little Cleeve – I was going to tell you about that. Toby left it in a disgraceful state and we have spent all this time putting it to rights. Now I think it looks very nice. Would you agree?'

'From what I saw of it, yes, and I congratulate you. I must also thank you.'

'What do you mean?' Sarah was genuinely puzzled.

'My father may not have received any rent these last years, but you have paid it twice over in the work you have done to keep the Grange in good order, the estate running nicely and Little Cleeve restored. I think I am in your debt rather than the other way round.'

She laughed. 'Not that argument again, I thought we had it settled. Though I must say that I am pleased to think that Marianne will enjoy some routs and parties in Anita's company and that she will be dressed as she should be.' She withdrew her hand from his. 'I have finished my story.'

'But you have not given me any advice.'

'What do you want me to say?'

'I want to know how I go about getting a new steward.' He stopped as with a sudden thought. 'Unless you are willing to go on doing it yourself, of course.'

She shook her head. 'Thank you for asking me, but I should ask the Humphries if I were you. I could not undertake it, I have received an offer of marriage, you see.' She saw a change in his expression. 'What is the matter?'

'You are going to accept it?'

'No, not yet. I am considering it. Are you surprised?' Sarah asked him. 'Did you think I was on the shelf and ripe for a flirtation?'

'You are a minx though you do not look like one. Your tongue betrays you.'

Sarah looked puzzled. 'I fail to understand myself. I have never been so rude to anyone in my life as I have been to you. It is just as though you bring out a devil in me.'

He smiled at her. 'I expect it is the rake in me,' he teased her. Then he looked at her carefully. 'And who is the gentleman? Is he a local person? Will I meet him?'

'Three questions: I will answer them one by one. He is Sir Bertram Hesslewood and he owns a big estate on the other side of Bidborough. He is older than I am but I have known him and his brother, Philip, all my life. Philip manages the estate for his brother. And yes, you are sure to meet him. He visits every day and was most kind the other day when I was confronted with our strange cousin at the Grange. In fact, I would not be surprised to find him safely established in the drawing-room when we return to the house.'

Her cousin stood up and offered her his arm. 'Let us go and meet this paragon and I will tell you if I approve of him as a husband for you.'

'And if you do not approve?' she asked him quizzically.

'I daresay I shall have to do something about it.'

'Odious man!'

He laughed again and they made their way back to the house.

In the drawing-room at Little Cleeve, the two girls were laughing at an out-of-date fashion book; Lady Hadlow still reclined on the *chaise-longue* and with her sat the very large man who was Sir Bertram Hesslewood. He turned to Sarah as she entered and rose rather peevishly.

'This is the second time I have found you missing lately, Sarah. Where have you been all this time?'

Sarah stood in shock: before her a man who suddenly seemed to be a country bumpkin of a person and none too pleasant; behind her, the elegant American who must have heard Sir Bertram's words.

She took a deep breath. 'Bertram, I am pleased to find you here for I wish to introduce you to our cousin from America. I have had a lot of business matters to discuss with him.' She turned back to Julian and received a further shock: dressed to a fault, he suddenly looked the dandy compared to the prosaic Sir Bertram. She pulled herself together for she must finish the introductions. 'Julian, this is Sir Bertram Hesslewood; he is the owner of Luttons Park and his land runs with ours – with yours, I should say. Bertram, I would like you to meet Mr Julian Cleeve of Cleeve Grange.'

The two men made their bows, the American's slight and graceful, Sir Bertram's stiff and awkward.

It was Julian who spoke first. 'Pleased to make your acquaintance, Hesslewood. May I wish you joy in your offer for Sarah?'

Sarah felt the blood rush to her head and face at the audacity of the remark, but the irony of it was lost on Sir Bertram who replied in a self-satisfied tone.

'Thank you, Cleeve. Sarah is a good girl. Have known her all my life, y'know. And it is about time I had an heir to the Hesslewood name. I must congratulate you on your daughter; nice little thing, she and Marianne are like sisters already.'

Julian Cleeve listened in silence then ignored Sir Bertram and stood beside Lady Hadlow. 'Cousin Mary, I have had a long talk with Sarah and I wish to make a suggestion. I need a companion for Anita and I would ask you if Marianne could come to live at Cleeve Grange and I will undertake to launch them both on the local ton I think you call it.'

'Papa.' His daughter jumped up in delight. 'There is nothing I would like better and you would, too, would you not, Marianne?' Anita turned to her new friend.

Marianne came forward shyly. 'I would like it above all things, Cousin Julian, but I am afraid I will have to decline.'

Julian's eyes sought Sarah's and she gave a slight nod. 'Marianne, I will be honest with you,' he said, 'then you will have no need to feel embarrassed. Sarah and I have had to make a business arrangement which I choose not to go into. Your sister knew that you would refuse to come to Cleeve Grange to be with Anita because of your inadequate wardrobe. Am I right?'

Marianne spoke sensibly. 'I have dresses enough to wear here at home which I have made myself. But I have not a single dress or gown that I could wear in Tunbridge Wells and not disgrace you or Anita.'

Julian thought it nicely said. 'You are not to worry your little head about such things. I shall have the dressing of the two of you; Sarah and I have agreed upon it. I somehow think that the first thing we must do from the look of it, is to get a new fashion book and find a mantua-maker – is that what you say? I am having to learn a lot of new words over here.'

They all laughed, except Sir Bertram who came forward and said in a blustering tone, 'Won't have it, Cleeve. It is my responsibility, or I am hoping it will be. I will provide any dresses or gowns that Marianne might need.'

Sarah stood between the two men and felt awkward. 'Bertram, I will explain it to you later. We are very much in my cousin's debt and I would be pleased to see Marianne accompany Anita to the Tunbridge Wells assemblies.'

Sir Bertram's face was red. 'Not happy at all, Sarah, but I will have to listen to you. I will come and see you in the morning. Must make my farewells now. Pleased to meet you Cleeve, and to have a Cleeve at the Grange once again. Goodbye, dear Lady Hadlow. It is good to see you in spirits once again.'

And with a bow to Sarah and Julian, he left the room and they heard the bang of the front door.

The silence that followed was quickly broken by Lady Hadlow, 'Dear Bertram, such a kind man. I am sure I do not know what we would do without him.'

Sarah looked at Julian, but she could not read his expression and she was glad to see her cousin turn to Anita.

'Come along, young lady, I am pleased you like our plans. Cousin Mary, we will come and fetch Marianne as soon as our carriage arrives. I am expecting it tomorrow.'

Later that same day found Sarah at the stables, for she knew she must speak to Philip about the arrangement with her cousin. She watched Reuben saddle Cilla, was handed up and set off at a gallop towards Luttons Park. As she went past the Grange gates, she saw two riders coming towards her from the direction of Luttons. She recognized immediately the tall, lean figure of Philip, but could see that it was not his brother with whom he was in conversation. Then, as they drew nearer, she realized with some astonishment that Philip was riding with her cousin.

Sarah reined Cilla in and waited. The two men were talking earnestly and laughing together.

Then Philip saw her. 'Sarah,' he called, and in seconds they were in a small group and Sarah was listening to their explanations.

Both men are handsome, there is no denying it, thought Sarah. Philip with serious good looks, intelligent blue eyes and classic features; Julian Cleeve the more flamboyant of the two, talking and laughing as though he had been forever acquainted with Philip Hesslewood.

'Cousin Sarah,' said Julian with little formality. 'Your Hesslewood friends are indeed kind. Philip learned from his brother that I had no mount as yet, and came to Cleeve Grange with this fine hunter for me. He has taken me round the Cleeve estate and shown me some of his own land. I am indebted to him.'

Sarah looked from one to the other feeling more than a little amused; she wondered what Philip would make of the American cousin who was so free in his manner.

'So it is one introduction that I do not have to make,' she smiled. 'You seem to be well acquainted already. May I join you?'

'I will leave you with your childhood sweetheart, Sarah.' Her cousin's tone was almost taunting and she stiffened slightly at his familiarity. 'I have left Anita on her own and I do not want her to be in a worry about me. As soon as our carriage arrives, I will come and fetch Marianne as we arranged. Goodbye, Hesslewood, and thank you again. Goodbye, Sarah, my sweet.'

He rode off quickly and Sarah, looking at Philip, expected laughter. But she could see from his face that he was displeased about something.

'What is it, Philip, does something trouble you? It was kind of you to take the hunter to the Grange. What do you make of my cousin?'

He moved his horse nearer to her and covered her hand with his; it was a natural gesture from Philip and Sarah was surprised at the sense of pleasure it gave her.

'I have a feeling that we cannot trust him, Sarah.'

She looked at him in astonishment. 'Whatever do you mean, Philip? I must admit to taking him in dislike when he first arrived, but he has been very understanding about the rents.' She told him quickly about the conversation she had had with Julian and its outcome. 'Did he tell you that Marianne is to go as companion to his daughter?'

'I appreciate that your problem over the rent is settled, but I dislike a man who is free in his speech and manner and laughs a lot and whose eyes remain cold and calculating. Almost as though he is saying one thing and thinking another. Did you not notice? And calling you "my sweet" when he has known you only a few days.'

'Philip.' Sarah replied hastily. 'This is not like you, surely you are not jealous?'

'No, of course I am not jealous, I have only known the man for an hour. If I ask you if he made you an object of his pleasantries this morning, I do believe you will say yes. Did he try a flirtation with you? He is the kind of man who would, and at the slightest provocation, too; and you are very lovely, Sarah.'

Sarah stared. Was this her Philip? But she was remembering Julian's offer to accept a kiss in payment for a debt when they were in the garden together and she coloured slightly.

Suddenly the old Philip was back and he laughed. 'I can tell he did. There is nothing I do not know about you, Sarah, my sweet.'

And Sarah joined in the laughter. 'You have never called me that, Philip, you are saying it just because Julian did.'

His reply was enigmatic. 'Perhaps I could learn a thing or two from him, Sarah; I think perhaps I have been slow. But watch your step with your cousin: I hardly know why I say it, it seems to be a sixth sense with me. Now let us forget the Julian Cleeves of this world – shall we have a gallop? . . . And, Sarah, you have not accepted my brother, have you? As much as I love you, I do not want you as a sister.'

And Sarah smiled as she led off across the fields; Philip had not been speaking of the kind of love she thought she would like to find one day. It made her wonder if it would ever be possible to find it with Philip himself. And what about the cousin whom Philip distrusted and who had been so suddenly catapulted into her life? He was an unknown quantity, but there was something about him that invited admiration and an easy friendship.

Four

OVER THE NEXT few weeks of May, there was both activity and laughter at Cleeve Grange. Marianne soon settled in and her youthful companionship was enjoyed by Anita who was one of those girls with pale complexion who looked rather plain when she was quiet, but as soon as she was in delight about something, her blue eyes would sparkle and she looked completely different. She looks quite grown up when she was enjoying herself with Marianne, Sarah had decided, and was pleased for both of them.

With Marianne gone and her mother still out of spirits – except when Bertram visited, Sarah noticed with an inward smile – the eldest of the Winterson children found herself at a loss.

She had no estate to manage and she missed her daily activities. It had been her hope that James would come home when he had taken his final examinations, but they had received a letter to say that he was going to enjoy a short break in Oxford. Sarah tried not to worry that he might turn after their father and take to the gaming tables.

She saw very little of her cousin who was occupied in learning his estate with his new steward. If they did meet, it usually occasioned a good-natured spat or a disagreement.

So, apart from the visits of Marianne and Anita, which she enjoyed, delighting in the change in her sister's fortunes, Sarah was left with the sole company of Sir Bertram. He arrived each day on his horse and would jog gently around the leafy lanes which led to the rolling parkland and the beautiful old manor house of Penshurst Place, built in 1340 and once the home of the poet, Sir Philip Sidney. Bertram would tell the history of the house and family every time they went in that direction. He did not seem to consider that she might enjoy a gallop and she guessed that he probably thought it unladylike to gallop across the fields.

Although Sarah enjoyed being out of the house, she had to endure long lectures from Bertram on the fitness of an American planter to be the new owner of Cleeve Grange. It was not like that when he had been a boy, he would tell her time and time again; the Cleeves had been a very respected Kentish family. Sarah had to bite her tongue not to make a swift retort in defence of her cousin.

Things went along in this way for over two weeks, with Sarah enduring Sir Bertram and seeing very little of Julian Cleeve, or even of Philip. She was at a loss to understand why she saw so little of Philip, who seemed to be deliberately avoiding her. She could not imagine that he was put out by the arrival of her cousin on the scene, though she remembered vividly how Philip had warned against Julian. And for very little reason, she would say to herself.

Even when Julian did come, it was usual to find Sarah's worthy suitor in possession of the drawing-room and he made a quick escape. His lack of civility was not lost on Sarah and it seemed inevitable that there should be another clash between them when he arrived one morning at an early hour and before the time of Bertram's daily visit.

He was shown in that morning and found Sarah alone in the drawing-room, Lady Hadlow being a late riser. He was right in thinking that Sarah was feeling less than her usual energetic and forceful self and he determined, even as she rose to greet him, to do something about it.

'Come for a ride with me,' he said. 'I am on Philip's hunter and

I could do with a companion, for I cannot persuade Anita to ride. Do come, Sarah.'

He was smiling at her and she thought he looked more handsome than ever. His riding coat was an exquisite fit over powerful shoulders and his breeches an extraordinary and unsuitable creamy-yellow. Sarah would have given anything to be able to say yes to his invitation, but there were two many obstacles.

'I would like to ride with you, Cousin,' she replied with some regret in her voice, 'but I am afraid I cannot.'

'Why not?'

'I have promised to ride with Bertram.'

He replied with little patience. 'But you go out riding with Hesslewood every day. I have often called in an afternoon and been told by your mama that you are out with him. Is it true that you are going to marry him?'

Sarah was immediately angry. 'And what has it to do with you whom I marry?'

'It has nothing to do with me. I feel I hardly know you and would like to know you better. And I might as well tell you that I do not wish to see you married to that hayseed of a bore called Hesslewood. Marry his brother if you like, though I understand he still grieves his wife; or marry me, Sarah. Would you marry me if I asked you? I think I might like a quick-tempered, shrewish cousin for a wife. What do you say?'

Sarah could hear the taunt in his voice and, when he put a hand on her arm and tried to draw her closer into his arms, she lost her temper and without thinking of anything but her cousin's insults, she raised her arm as though to hit him.

Sarah was a tall girl, and she was strong; she had taken her cousin by surprise, but he caught hold of the raised arm, at the same time making a grab for her waist and pulling her up close to him. His lips were on hers and he forced his kiss on her. For one second, Sarah was lost, for no one had ever kissed her in such a way and she felt a quick rush of passion that was almost a desire to return the embrace.

But she wrenched herself free, at the back of her mind hearing Philip's voice telling her not to trust her cousin.

'You are no gentleman, Cousin; are you in the habit of kissing any lady you might meet? And is my Marianne safe with you?'

And Sarah knew she had gone too far.

He gripped her arms with strong fingers and she could see anger in his eyes. 'You choose to insult me, Cousin. If I am no gentleman then you are no lady to suggest that I do not know how to behave with a young girl as sweet as Marianne. I wait for your apology.'

Sarah sat down suddenly. They had been standing by the ottoman in the window of the drawing-room and knowing she had behaved badly, she felt the need to sit and not to confront him again. She had never met any gentleman quite like her Cousin Julian; she knew that somehow they would always be at daggers drawn but some perverse emotion in her felt his attraction.

She lifted her head at last and found that he was looking down at her with an odd smile; she was unable to tell what he was thinking. 'I am sorry, Julian. I am sure that Marianne is both safe and happy at Cleeve Grange with you and Anita.'

'And I apologize for the kiss. Could you not think again and come riding with me? Sir Bertram has not appeared and I am sure Cousin Mary will be pleased to entertain him if he does come.'

She looked at him suspiciously. 'And what is that supposed to mean?'

'Have you not seen, my little goose, that the estimable Sir Bertram would make a better partner for your mama than for yourself?'

Sarah sighed. 'I have thought of it and I must tell you that I have no intention of accepting his offer. But I do not think he would turn to Mama; he needs an heir, you see.'

Julian surprised her by roaring with laughter. 'That is not lady-like, Cousin. I have an idea that you should not mention such things in polite society.'

Sarah smiled at last for she knew he was right. 'You bring out the worst in me, Cousin; perhaps it is because I do not consider you to be polite society.'

'Shrew. Now I demand your company for a ride.'

Sarah got up knowing that he had won her over. 'Very well, I will change into my riding-habit and join you at the stables. I had better warn you that my riding dress is quite old and shabby.'

'I do not believe it,' he replied. 'I will have a chat with your mama for I think she is about to join us. But do not take hours changing, if you please.'

'Of course I won't; do you take me for a dilly-dallier, always in front of the looking-glass trying to decide what to wear?'

'I take you for a woman of good sense and charm,' he said.

'Balderdash; doing it too brown, Cousin. I might have sense but little charm, as you have discovered.'

'You do not know yourself, my peagoose.'

'I am not your . . . oh, fiddle, I will go and change. There you are, Mama,' she said, as Lady Hadlow entered the room. 'Cousin Julian has tempted me to ride with him. Do explain to Bertram if he comes.' And she hurried upstairs to change.

Julian kissed Lady Hadlow on the cheek as she entered the drawing-room.

She smiled at him. 'Do not scold me for not rising earlier, Julian. I am permitted to be lazy at my age. Can I offer you some coffee?'

'No, thank you, Cousin Mary. I do not think that Sarah will be very long. She was half-expecting Sir Bertram but he has not appeared.'

Lady Hadlow nodded. 'It may be the afternoon before he comes. I live in hope that he will persuade Sarah to marry him. Dear Bertram.'

He looked at her searchingly. 'You are pleased with the match, Cousin Mary?'

Her smile told of her reply. 'Yes indeed. Sarah is very fortunate. Such a worthy gentleman and so very kind. He comes and chats with me for an age before going riding with Sarah in the afternoons. I think sometimes I might have fallen in love with him had I been younger.'

Julian had to swallow hard to maintain his grave expression. 'But you and Hesslewood are very close in age,' he said to her.

She gave what could only be described as a simpering smile. 'He is a year older than me, but I pride myself on looking younger – when I am not cast-down, that is. Bertram has chosen Sarah and I must be thankful. She dotes on him, you know. There was never anyone else for Sarah. Philip is more of an age with Sarah, but he still mourns his young wife and has always been as a brother to Sarah.'

It was fortunate for Julian's composure that Sarah chose that moment to enter the room. He thought she looked becoming and said so. Her riding-habit was of a dull red with grey frogging and her riding hat was black with a dashing feather.

'You told me the lie about your riding-dress, Sarah, you look charming.'

'No, Julian, you cannot fool or flatter me. My habit might still fit me well, but I have worn it these eight years and it can only be described as dowdy.'

'Balderdash, as you are fond of saying. Let us go.'

Round at the stables, Julian handed her up on Cilla and they rode off in the direction of Cleeve Grange.

Anita and Marianne came to the front door of the Grange and were admiring. 'How nice to see you out riding with Papa,' said Anita. 'I still like horses, but I just do not seem to have the courage to get on one.'

'You will one day, Anita,' said Sarah with a smile. 'It will happen all of a sudden and you will be pleased with yourself.'

Julian rode up to them. He had been having a quick word with John Capel, who was his new steward.

'Are you fit, young lady? Shall we go up to Blackthorn Wood?'

'Yes, please,' Sarah answered readily and they were off.

It was hilly country around Bidborough, and behind Cleeve Grange, the land rose gently upwards towards a small wood; it had always been a favourite ride for Sarah.

She gave Cilla her head but she could not keep up with Julian who had galloped a long way in front of her.

When Sarah arrived exhilarated at the trees, he had dismounted and was waiting for her.

'That was glorious,' Sarah said. 'Cilla enjoyed it too, Julian, but I could not catch you.'

He smiled at her and held out his arms. 'Jump,' he ordered.

And instead of being handed down politely, Sarah did as she was bidden. She jumped and was then held fast in his arms.

'I think I would like a cousinly kiss,' he murmured close to her ear.

'You do not get any kind of kiss. It is a dangerous practice.'

'I like danger,' he smiled.

'Trust you to twist my meaning,' she replied quickly.

He took no notice of her remark and looked down at her, suddenly serious. 'Sarah, I think in good time, I will buy ponies for Anita and Marianne. I believe that is the way to get Annie's confidence back.'

'Annie?' she questioned with a frown. 'You mean Anita?'

There was a moment's hesitation, and she was unable to read the expression on his face; if anything, she thought he looked annoyed with himself. But his answer came with his usual broad smile. 'Yes, Annie is my pet name for her whenever we are on our own. But Anita is a nice name and she does not like me to shorten it . . . what do you think about the ponies?' he added with a deft change of subject.

'I think it both wise and practical and I will help if I can.'

'Bless you . . . now I think we must ride back. We will go more gently this time. Let me hand you up and we will be off. Will you come again tomorrow?'

Back on Cilla, Sarah smiled down at him. 'Maybe, Cousin, maybe.'

At Cleeve Grange, they parted and Julian went in search of Anita and Marianne. Outside the drawing-room, he was amazed to find Marianne at the pianoforte and Anita singing quite sweetly. He paused for a moment before opening the door and going in.

'Don't stop,' he said to them as he entered. 'That was very nice. What gave you the idea?'

Anita came up and gave him a kiss. 'Marianne has been trying to teach me the pianoforte, but I am rather a duffer at it so she suggested we tried some songs. We found some old song sheets and Marianne says that I sing very nicely.'

'I think so, too,' agreed her father and then turned to Marianne. 'Tell me, Marianne, what do you make of your prospective brother-in-law?'

'Bertram?' She was silent for a long time before she spoke. 'I will have to be honest, I cannot dissemble but I will try not to be rude. He is always polite, he is kind and pleasant to Mama which I do appreciate, but apart from that I consider him to be a dull stick and a bore. How Sarah can contemplate being married to him, I fail to understand. I only hope that she will refuse him and that she is not tempted into marriage with him in order to give me a season and Mama a home at Luttons Park.' She paused and looked at Anita. 'And Anita agrees with me. We have tried to think of plans for getting Bertram together with Mama, but I am afraid we are at a loss.'

Anita chipped in, 'Perhaps you could do something about it, Papa.'

He looked at her with a mischievous smile. 'Perhaps I could,' was all he said.

Back at Little Cleeve, Sarah was going over that morning's conversation with her cousin, then thinking about Philip and his odd silence, when Bertram arrived.

For once, he had not ridden but had arrived in a stylish curricle not at all suited to his middle-aged demeanour, which was drawn by two spirited greys of which he was very proud. He said he thought it made him look younger, but Sarah considered it made him look a ridiculous figure in the narrow country lanes around Bidborough.

However, she never objected to riding with him for he was a first-class whip and knew his horses well.

Sarah was sitting in the drawing-room with her mother when he arrived and, as usual, she could not help making the contrast between the elegant Julian and the cumbersome Sir Bertram, that day dressed soberly in fawn breeches and a dull-brown riding coat with a modest two capes.

He bowed to them both. 'Sarah, my dear. And, Mary, you look as lovely as ever.' This last to Lady Hadlow whom he had always addressed by her first name in a rather intimate fashion which Lady Hadlow seemed to revel in.

'Dear Bertram, you never miss a day. How nice to see you and in your curricle today, too.'

Bertram turned to Sarah. 'I have a commission in Tunbridge Wells, Sarah and, as there is something I wish to speak to you about, perhaps you will not object to accompanying me in the curricle.'

Sarah's heart sank, she could guess what the 'something' was and steeled herself to give him a more outright refusal even though she was still wondering if she should accept Bertram for her mother's sake. He had always promised Lady Hadlow a home at Luttons Park when she needed it and it seemed to Sarah that she must consider her mother's welfare as well as her own happiness.

But she replied brightly enough. 'Certainly, Bertram, I would enjoy a visit to the Wells and perhaps you would not object if I made some purchases at the linen-drapers while we are there. I find I am running short of tapestry wools.'

Bertram was all compliance; the thought of a wife at Luttons Park busy at her tapestry seemed a very satisfactory and promising notion.

It was a warm day but overcast and Sarah wore a light pelisse of cream moiré silk over her cotton dress; her bonnet was also cream and decorated with pale green ribbons. She looked becoming and old-fashioned at the same time and Bertram felt proud of her.

He drove at a slow pace down the lane which would take them to Bidborough before joining the turnpike road into the town.

'Sarah,' Bertram started to say and she knew he was going to be very formal. 'You know of my feelings and my wishes with regard to you becoming my wife. It is several months since I first made my declaration and I feel that the time has come to ask you for a definite acceptance and for us to plan our marriage and the removal of you and your mama to Luttons Park. Now that Marianne is settled with your cousin and James will soon be starting his diplomatic career, you have no need to be troubled on their behalf. We will be in Brighton as usual in August, for our house has been settled on since last year and I think we all enjoy those weeks in the sea air, with all the entertainments which the Regent has to offer at the Marine Pavilion . . . did you say something, Sarah?'

'No, no,' she hastened to reply and wondered if her wicked thought that he was never going to finish had in fact been said aloud.

'When we return from Brighton, the hunting season will soon be with us; I like to think that we could arrange our marriage and honeymoon in September and be home in time for me to follow the hounds as I always do. So if you could let me have your answer within the next day or so, I would be most grateful, and your mama and 1 can begin to plan for the event.'

Sarah felt as though she had been turned to stone. All this had been said to her in Bertram's flat monotone and with him not looking at her once but keeping his eyes on his horses.

'You are silent, Sarah. Do not rush, my dear, for I know it is an important decision for you.'

Sarah's only thought was that she could not do it. I cannot marry him, the words seemed to cry out inside her, I cannot. I would rather spend the rest of my life as a spinster at Little Cleeve looking after Mama and being an aunt to Marianne's children for she is so pretty she is bound to marry.

Bertram continued, 'I expect I have surprised you with talking of the plans which must be made, so I will ask for your reply tomorrow, Sarah. Talk it over with your dear mama and see what she has to say.'

'I cannot marry you, Bertram. I am grateful for your offer but I must decline.' The words were forced, stilted.

'Eh, what is that you say? You cannot decline, Sarah, I have waited all this time for you. I hope that ill-mannered cousin of yours has not put unseemly ideas into your head.'

'Julian has been very kind to us and especially to Marianne. He has nothing to do with the matter.'

'That is all right then, have a talk with Mary and give me your answer tomorrow . . . now, here we are at the turnpike and I must keep my eye on the road. I will look forward to your decision Sarah.'

Sarah sat up as stiff as a ramrod and with no expression on her face. Inside she could feel rebellion and she almost wished that it was Julian who was asking for her hand. She felt a longing for a talk with Philip, he would know what to say.

She could hardly recall the rest of the trip into the town; she purchased her wools, rejoined Bertram and they drove home again with Bertram talking endlessly about his friendship with the Regent and how he looked forward to his weeks in Brighton.

That evening after dinner, Sarah knew at last that there was only one thing she could do: and that was to seek Philip out.

On Cilla's back once again, she rode quickly over the fields to Luttons Park. She smiled as she reached the dower house for in its outside appearance it was not unlike Little Cleeve and had been built at the same time. Inside, it had larger rooms and was more elegant in its furnishings and drapes.

When Clara had died, Mrs Bainbridge, their cook, had stayed on as both cook and housekeeper to Philip and took care of him as though he was still a little boy. She even called him 'Master Philip' on occasions when she was not thinking. It always amused Sarah.

She found Philip just finishing his dinner and he was pleased to see her.

'Sarah, my sweet friend, this is an honour. Can I get you a glass of sherry, or would you join me in the port? It is too early for the tea-tray to be brought in.' He led her through to the drawing-room and they sat together on a long sofa strewn with comfortable cushions; the sight of them always made Sarah feel sad for she could so clearly remember Clara sitting quietly making the covers before her lying-in.

'I will have a glass of sherry, if you please, Philip. And I must tell you that I have come to reproach you.'

He looked at her half-seriously. 'Whatever can you mean? Surely we are the best of friends.'

'Yes, of course we are, but if that is so, why is it that you have been avoiding me for the last week or two?'

He gave a laugh and she could hear mischief in it. 'So you noticed? You flatter me, Sarah. Did you not realize that I would want to leave the field clear for my big brother?'

Sarah stared. 'You cannot mean it. I have been pestered with Bertram's attentions all this time and you must know that your brother is not the most scintillating of company. Why, you won't even live in the same house as him.'

Philip leaned forward and took her hand in his. 'My greatest wish is to see you happy, Sarah. I thought perhaps it would please you to be Lady Hesslewood and to live at Luttons Park and to be able to take your mama with you.'

'No, it does not please me and I have told him so today. But he does not seem to be able to take no for an answer; he is already planning a marriage and a honeymoon in September before the hunting season begins . . . oh, you might laugh,' she said, for Philip had burst into hearty laughter.

'Sarah, you must see it. Which is the more important to Bertram, you or the hounds? You will have to say no, won't you? How are you going to convince him?'

'I do not know, you tell me.'

'You could tell him you are going to marry me, Sarah.'

Sarah could tell that he said it in fun and said so. 'Now you are roasting me; you know very well that you always say that you will never replace Clara and Bertram knows it, too. Can you not think of something more convincing?'

Philip was still holding her hand and he raised it to his lips. 'I think I would like to kiss you,' he said softly.

Sarah felt nothing but outrage and her tongue was unguarded. 'Oh, not you as well,' she said, more sharply than she had meant to.

He held on to her hand tightly and she could feel an unexpected tension in him. 'And what does that mean? I suppose you have been accepting kisses from the American cousin. I hear that you have been riding with him.'

'No, I have not been accepting Julian's kisses. He asked for a cousinly kiss and I refused.'

'You mean he did not force his attentions on you?'

'No, of course he did not. He is a gentleman.'

Philip stood up and Sarah could not believe the sternness and bitterness of his expression. 'Julian Cleeve is no gentleman, of that I am certain. There is something havey-cavey about him though I am sure I do not know what it is.'

Sarah was angry and she stood up and faced her old friend. 'You say that because you are jealous, Philip Hesslewood. You leave me alone for two weeks and then take me to task over my cousin who has been very kind to us. And I might tell you that his behaviour is beyond reproach.'

'Well, mine is not,' said Philip gruffly, and he seized her somewhat violently and pulled her into his arms.

Sarah was so surprised at Philip's action that she did not begin to struggle and when she felt his lips on hers, she was seized with a breathless wish to surrender to him.

She was released suddenly and looked up into angry eyes. 'Now you can say that I am not a gentleman,' he said in a tone that was far from pleasant.

'I will not say anything to you except goodbye. You have been absent from Little Cleeve for over two weeks and you can stay away for another two weeks for all I care.'

And Sarah rushed from the room and out of the house, brushing her angry tears from her eyes and trying to make sense of her turbulent feelings.

The following day, she still could not forget Philip's behaviour – that was until Julian appeared for their morning ride.

Julian had been discussing the plans for the come-out ball with Anita and Marianne and was keen to speak to Lady Hadlow.

The two girls had asked him if he had any thoughts about the come-out and he had to confess to them that he had not.

They were sitting at breakfast when Anita mentioned it and he looked from one to the other. 'I have not spoken about it to either the Humphries or to Lady Hadlow. Have you two rascals been putting your heads together about it? You had better tell me.'

Anita gave a pleased laugh. 'We have talked about it and have made all sorts of plans, but we thought it too soon to mention it to you.'

'Out with it then.'

Anita spoke for them both. 'Jane Humphries is having her come-out ball at the Assembly Rooms on her eighteenth birthday, that is June 20th. We wondered if the three of us could make our come-out together. That is if the Humphries would agree to it; Jane loves the idea. And I won't have a ball unless Marianne is included, Papa.'

Anita and Marianne were firm friends of Jane's. The three of them were much of an age and were also the same height and slender build; two of them were fair and one dark and they always made a pretty and intriguing trio.

Julian was smiling thoughtfully. 'I think it is a very nice idea and I will see Sir Roger; we will try and arrrange it between us. It is time the invitations were sent out, I should think. I am just going down to Little Cleeve and I will mention it to Cousin Mary.'

At Little Cleeve, Lady Hadlow was delighted with the idea and would talk of nothing else. But when Sarah appeared, she was less than interested and Julian thought she seemed distracted about something.

They walked round to the stables together, saying very little; then, as he handed Sarah down when they reached the wood, Julian looked at her searchingly.

'What is all this about?' Julian asked her. 'You are gloomy and your thoughts are far away. That is not like you.'

Sarah managed a bleak smile. 'I am sorry, Cousin, it is something that happened yesterday.'

'Are you going to tell me? Let us walk into the trees and find somewhere to sit.' And they left the horses to graze and walked into the wood, finding several fallen trees and mossy trunks to sit on. 'Sarah, you are troubled and although I would like to kiss that little frown away, I promise I will not.'

'Does it show?'

'I think I could sense you were unhappy if I were a mile away. What is it?' He possessed himself of her hand and that was the only contact between them. Sarah had taken off her riding gloves and was glad to cling to him as it was not easy to explain her disordered throughts. She also knew that it was not proper of her to talk him in the first place, but he was her cousin and who else did she have to advise her now that Philip seemed to be lost to her?

'It is Bertram.' She found that it was all she could say.

'I thought as much. What has the nodcock done now? Not by any good chance turned you off and made an offer for your mama, has he?'

Sarah laughed then and she had thought she would never laugh again. 'Oh, Julian, you are preposterous. Are you never serious? We either fight or laugh, you must admit it.'

'I will admit to the fact that you arouse many emotions in me, Cousin. You make me angry; you make me laugh; you make me want to protect you; and you make me want to kiss you.'

'Julian, you promised,' she said hastily.

'I am going to keep my promise, ma'am.' He raised her hand to his lips. 'There, that will suffice. Now tell me about the estimable Bertram.'

'He insists on me giving him a reply. He wants to marry me before the hunting season begins.'

'Are you really serious, Sarah, do you love the man?'

'No.' It was said emphatically.

'Then do not marry him. He will not do for you, I have said that before. What about Philip? I have asked you that, too.'

Sarah's face was both sad and worried. 'Philip and I have quarrelled.'

'You have quarrelled? May I ask the cause of the disagreement?'

'It is you.'

'You have quarrelled over me? And what is that supposed to mean? Philip hardly knows me.' Julian looked down at the troubled girl he was coming to know so well.

'I said that to him, but he is acting as though he is jealous and it does not make any sense.'

Five

JULIAN CLEEVE AND Sarah sat silent for a few moments in the wood, both of them busy with their own thoughts.

When Julian at last spoke, it was with a measured carefulness quite unlike him. 'Sarah, I have to tell you that Philip has cause for jealousy.'

She looked at him, startled. 'Whatever can you mean?'

'How long have I known you, Sarah? Not a lot more than a month? In that short space of time, I have seen you almost every day and some of that time in Sir Bertram's company. I will not speak of love, Sarah, but I have become more than fond of you and not just in a cousinly sense. And because of that, I would not like seeing you married to Bertram. He is not the man for you, and if his brother has not come up to scratch, then I want to ask you if you would do me the honour of becoming my wife.'

Sarah's mind went into an instant whirl. 'What . . . whatever are you saying, Julian?' It was not like Sarah to stammer, but he had taken her so completely by surprise that her tongue seemed to be unable to find any sensible words.

'Sarah, I can tell that I have surprised you. But have you not seen my regard? Have you not realized that I have so often wanted to take you in my arms and to kiss you? Think, Sarah, are we not right for one another? We do clash, I know that, but I enjoy our good-tempered badinage. You are not afraid to say what you think and I like that in a girl. No simpering misses for me, thank you.'

Sarah was sitting in her favourite place amongst the trees of Blackthorn Wood but she saw no trees. She was listening to Julian's voice, she was looking at him, but it was not his face she saw: it was Philip's, so angry the night before. But Philip still belonged to Clara and was not for her even though he had shown an unusual animosity towards Julian and Julian's attentions.

Marry Julian? She asked herself . . . I like him, and we could move back to Cleeve Grange; he is wealthy, not that wealth is important to me; I might come to love him in time. But most of all, was her final thought before speaking again, I could forget about Bertram.

And those were her first words to Julian. 'I could forget about Bertram.'

'Precisely, my love. Has your wise little head at last worked out the advantages? I cannot marry for a few months because it is less than a year since Lucy died, but a betrothal would be enough to keep Hesslewood from under your feet. It might even send him into your dear mother's arms.'

Sarah laughed then. 'Julian Cleeve, have you plotted all this to make a match between Mama and Bertram, or do you really wish to marry me?'

He put his hands on her arms. 'Yes, I find that I would like to marry you, my goose. Are you able to give me a reply, or do you wish to think about it? Please say yes, for it means I will be able to kiss you.'

'Would you still want to marry me if I refused to kiss you?'

'Minx,' he smiled. 'I daresay I could wait for the kiss, but I don't think you would deny me . . . let us try to see if it will help you make up your mind.'

'I think my mind is made up.'

'Does that mean you will accept me and my kiss?' Julian spoke with a jest in his voice and Sarah felt a relief that he was not being too serious.

'I am not thinking of kisses, I am thinking of the advantages of being marrried to you. It seems to me that the advantages are all on my side, Cousin.'

'On the other hand, Sarah, it means I can settle into Cleeve Grange with a beautiful young wife at my side.'

'Flattery will get you nowhere, Julian. My looks are no more than ordinary as you are well aware.'

His hands moved to her shoulders. 'To me you are both good-looking and sharp-witted and that adds up to being beautiful. Now say yes, you will become my wife.'

Sarah was very tempted. It might be that love had passed her by, but she liked her cousin and it would seem a very advantageous match.

She lifted her head to give him his reply and might have known what the result would be. He pulled her closely to him and his lips claimed hers; it was not a lingering or passionate kiss, and if her feelings were not stirred as they had been by Philip's embrace, neither did she feel any urge to withdraw from him.

'You have said yes, Sarah.'

Sarah had indeed made up her mind and became very serious. 'Thank you for you kind offer, Cousin. I accept it gladly.'

He jumped up with seeming delight. 'Well done, let us ride back and tell your mama.'

'And Bertram,' replied Sarah with some glee.

But when they arrived back at Little Cleeve, it was to find the Hesslewood horses in the stables and both Bertram and Philip entertaining Lady Hadlow.

Sarah thought she imagined that the Hesslewood brothers both stiffened into formality when she entered the drawing-room on Julian's arm.

'Hesslewood, Philip.' He bowed and turned to Lady Hadlow. 'And Cousin Mary; I have some news for you. Sarah has done me the honour of saying that she would like to become my wife; I ask your permission as head of the family and hope you will congratulate us.'

Sarah afterwards thought that if she had been a bystander, the ensuing minutes would have been nothing more than a pantomime.

There was an ominous silence for what seemed a long moment and Sarah, looking at the Hesslewoods, saw a stupified Bertram and an enraged Philip.

The silence was broken by a shrill cry from Lady Hadlow. Bertram rushed to her side, holding her in his arms to prevent her from going into a swoon and shouting at Julian and Sarah at the same time. Sarah had never heard his voice raised in all the time she had known him.

'So this is what has been going on behind my back! Cousins indeed! More like lovers I should think and riding together every morning. My eyes have been opened! It was no wonder you would give me no reply, Sarah! As for you, Cleeve, and your rakish American ways. . . .'

But they never did find out what Bertram thought of the rakish American for Lady Hadlow gave a scream and clung to Bertram.

'Bertram,' she cried out to him. 'You must marry Sarah, or I will lose you as a son and that I could not bear.'

He went on his knees in front of her and took her hands in his. 'My dearest Mary, you will not lose me at all for I have always loved you sincerely and you will gain me as a husband. It will be a privilege to ask you to marry me and to let me take care of you for the rest of my life.'

'Dear Bertram,' said Lady Hadlow and fainted away into his arms.

Sarah herself, speechless at her mother's behaviour and still holding Julian's arm, was alarmed at Philip's expression: his face had gone white and his lips were pressed tightly together. His hands were clenched and for a moment, she thought he was going to hit out at Julian.

Only Julian was unmoved. He watched the scene before him with gratification, as if he had achieved his aim sooner than he had expected. He bent to speak to Sarah. 'I will go and fetch Anita and Marianne, they must be part of the celebration, my sweet.'

And Sarah nodded dumbly as he went out of the room and she was left with a Philip who seemed beside himself with rage.

He came up to her and clasped her by the arm. 'Come into the garden with me, I must speak with you,' he said grimly.

Seeing that her mama and Bertram were engrossed with each other, Sarah had no option but to be led into the garden by the angry Philip. She had no wish to have a public quarrel with him.

They did not reach the end of the garden. Behind the first tall rhododendron bush and out of the sight of the house, Philip took her in his arms and kissed her. All his angry passion went into that kiss and Sarah found herself clinging to him and returning the kiss with feelings she had never experienced before.

But he suddenly let her go and she would have fallen back if his hand had not been still holding her around the waist.

'Now tell me you don't love me. What is this ridiculous story of being engaged to marry your cousin? You know very well that I would have married you to save you from Bertram's clutches. What do you mean by it?'

Sarah was bewildered, shaken by passion and angry all at the same time. And she shouted back at him.

'I have accepted Julian's offer because he made it. Last night you chose to be jealous; you joked with me about marrying you when we all know how you feel about Clara. I respected that you could not feel it proper to replace Clara in your life, for she was the sweetest girl I have ever known. You had no real wish to marry me and Julian did, so I accepted him. There is nothing you can do about it, for I am sure I will be happy with him. He is both charming and thoughtful and his offer has already had the effect of bringing Mama and Bertram together.'

'You do not love him,' he said, in a taciturn voice.

'No, maybe I do not love him, but I like him and we do well together. That is all I ask.'

'Is it? You would deny the friendship of a lifetime for a wolf in sheep's clothing from America?'

'What in the world do you mean by that remark, sir?'

He spoke reluctantly. 'I was not going to tell you for I cannot begin to work it out for myself. But on two occasions recently, I have been out before breakfast and have seen your cousin on his hunter riding with Anita on a spendid grey in the direction of Luttons. He pretends that Anita is frightened by her fall and will not ride. What does that mean?'

Sarah spoke impatiently. 'You are making something out of nothing. Julian has been trying persuade Anita on to a horse again; perhaps he feels he will have more success when they are quietly on their own.' Even as she said the words, a little niggling remembrance came to her of Julian saying he would buy ponies for Anita and Marianne. But she dismissed the thought immediately; maybe her cousin had got Anita to try to ride again in the last few days. 'And it is obvious that Anita was in an accident, for sometimes she limps quite badly. I think it is when her leg is paining her.'

'You are quick to spring to his defence, Sarah. I will wish you happy with him though it hurts me to say so. Please give my excuses to your mama, I must get back to Luttons.'

And she watched him stalk off to the stables, tall and purposeful.

She gave a sigh. I have lost him and I feel bereft, but I hope I have done the right thing, she murmured to herself as she walked back into Little Cleeve. I have no wish to upset Philip, I love him too much for that – and she stopped short. What have I said? Then she dismissed the thought from her mind for she knew very well that she had always loved Philip as a very dear brother.

It is true that if Philip had made me an offer before Bertram had decided to do so, and before Julian Cleeve had arrived on the scene, I would have been happy to accept him – even if it had meant taking second place to Clara.

Now it is Julian who has rescued me from my indecision about Bertram, she told herself firmly, and it is Julian I will marry. We have often clashed but there is no doubt about his good intentions.

Suddenly, Sarah felt happier about the future of all her family. Mama and Bertram at Luttons Park, Marianne at Cleeve Grange with Anita and once I am married to Julian, I will be returning there as his wife. There was a lingering ache in her heart over Philip, but she tried to dismiss it and dwell on the benefits that Julian Cleeve had brought to them all.

The next day, the quarrel between Sarah and Philip was entirely forgotten in the homecoming of Sarah's brother, James, the young Lord Hadlow. Sarah had been expecting him for many weeks. She knew that his time at Oxford was finished for he had written to tell them of securing his degree with honours and his wish to stay on there for a short while.

In the afternoon, and by now it was early June, there was a steady downpour and it was considered too wet to ride. Instead, Julian had brought Anita and Marianne over to Little Cleeve in the carriage and they were all in the drawing-room. Sarah had joined the younger girls and their cousin in a crazy game of Speculation in which they were trying to teach Julian the intricacies of the betting. He declared it to be more complicated than whist and this statement was to much laughter.

It was on this scene with a contented Lady Hadlow sitting with her hand in Bertram's, that the door burst open and a tall, handsome young man entered followed by a lady who could only be described as vulgar.

James – for indeed it was the young Lord Hadlow – stood tall and proud. He looked older than his twenty-one years and was dressed to a fault but not at all the dandy. His coat was of blue superfine, his pantaloons white over gleaming Hessians, and if his waistcoat could be described as a showy canary yellow, then his shirt points were only moderately high and his neck-cloth lightly starched and carefully arranged.

It was the expression in his eyes that one would notice; set in a finely drawn face under raven-black hair, they were that day, brilliant and defiant.

He had his hand on his companion's arm and he was laughing down at her. 'Come in, Crystal my dear, and meet my family . . . and I do believe that my American cousins are here, too. Mama, I have brought Miss Crystal de Florette to meet you; we hope to marry soon. I must tell you that Crystal is a famous actress in Oxford and in London, too.'

There was a silence that could only be described as awful in the drawing-room of Little Cleeve as Crystal de Florette took a step forward towards Lady Hadlow. That the actress was beautiful could not be denied, but it was a kind of beauty carefully adorned. Her very fair hair was piled high to make her nearly as tall as James and it was crowned by a concoction of plumes and ribbons of a gaudy red and purple. Her travelling dress was also purple; a stiff satin with edges of white fur round the full sleeves and the hem. Around her neck hung a rope of very large, ostentatious pearls which Sarah – who was staring at the newcomer in astonishment – knew must be artificial.

But Sarah was also thinking that all that might have been excused if Miss Florette had not spoken. She stood by the *chaise-longue* and laughed down at the stricken Lady Hadlow who winced even at the very first words which the actress spoke in a coarse and jocular tone.

'Oh la, Lady Hadlow. I am so pleased because you are going to be my mama-in-law and, of course, I will be Lady Hadlow. I never thought to marry a lord, indeed I didn't, but as soon as I met James, I knew he was the one for me. And here you are settled in your lovely little house and James has told me all about Cleeve Grange. He does love the place so, don't you, James?'

Not a word came from any occupant of that room. Sarah could not believe what was happening and thought she must be either watching a pantomime or living through a nightmare. She was wishing that Philip was there but there was no sign of him that day and she looked at Julian in desperation; their eyes met and he immediately jumped to his feet.

'I am indeed Julian Cleeve, the American cousin, and I am staying at Cleeve Grange while I am in England. Cousin James, I am pleased to meet you. Miss Florette, may I congratulate you and welcome you to the family. Now, I must tell you that Lady Hadlow is not at all the thing and must be spared any excitement at all costs for fear it should bring on one of her nervous spasms. She has only yesterday become betrothed to Sir Bertram Hesslewood, I am pleased to say.' Julian did not look at Sarah but turned to James. 'Cousin James, I expect you had forgot that there would not be a spare bedroom here at Little Cleeve for Miss Florette. I will take her back to the Grange with me where she will be more comfortable and you may visit as often as you wish.'

James stammered a reply. 'Thank you, Cousin, it is kind indeed and I would like Crystal to see the Grange straight away.' He went over to his mother. 'Mama, I am sorry to see you laid low, but I am pleased about your betrothal. I had thought Bertram was to marry Sarah. I will come and be quiet with you in a moment.'

He then turned to the young people still seated at the card table. 'Marianne, it is good to see you again and. . . .' He hesitated as he saw Anita. 'I know, you must be Anita. Mama wrote and told me you were here with Cousin Julian and that Marianne was your companion. I am pleased to meet you.'

Then he saw that Julian was at the door, Crystal at his side and he hurried over to them.

'Crystal, do go to the Grange with my cousin. I will pay off the cab and follow in a little while when I have told Mama all about us . . . the rain is not as heavy as it was.'

And the charade is over, thought Sarah, as she watched them go. She was furiously angry with Julian for making James's dreadful companion so welcome. It was very much a match that would not do for a Winterson; what in the world is James thinking of? She found the vinaigrette and hurried to her mother's side and gave it to Bertram.

'Sarah . . . Bertram,' gasped Lady Hadlow. 'James cannot marry a woman like that. What are we to do?'

'Do not worry, Mama,' replied Sarah sounding more calm than she felt. 'I will have a word with James, he must have taken leave of his senses. And Cousin Julian has not helped matters except that he has at least removed her to the Grange. I suppose that is something to be thankful for.' She turned as James came back into the room. 'James, has she gone? Whatever are you thinking of? You cannot marry such a woman. You are Lord Hadlow.'

James stood stiffly. 'You are judging by appearances. Crystal may not dress quite the lady, but she is truly very beautiful and sweet-natured, too. Could you not see that? And I must say that Cousin Julian has turned up trumps in taking het to the Grange like that. Is he going to be long in England? How soon will you be able to go back to the Grange? I must say that I had forgotten how small Little Cleeve was, but I daresay we will manage for a while, you seem very cosy.'

Sarah hardly knew what to say for James seemed to be under a misapprehension about his cousin and the Grange. 'I must tell you, James, that I am engaged to marry our cousin.'

James was startled. 'Good God – I mean congratulations, Sarah, that is splendid news. Does it mean you will go back to America with him? I do not think that Mama would care for that.'

'But, James . . .' Sarah started to say, but he was already talking to Anita and Marianne.

'Marianne, you are prettier than ever, in fact the two of you make a pretty pair. I suppose you must be bosom bows by now.'

It was Anita who replied. 'James, you cannot marry an actress. It is not done in America and I am sure it is not the thing here in England.'

Sarah looked at her with a little smile of amusement. Anita had dared to express the sentiments the Wintersons had thought, but had not the nerve to say.

James stood by the card table. 'You are very outspoken, Anita, is that the American way? I quite like it. But Crystal will no longer be an actress when we are married. I am entering the diplomatic service, you know.'

Sarah, standing with Bertram and Lady Hadlow, and having failed in her attempt to make James understand about the Grange, almost choked with laughter. The thought of Crystal de Florette in a colonial embassy was almost too much for anyone's composure.

He is no more than a young boy, she was saying to herself. I will have to try and convince him that she will not do. But it is not going to be easy if Julian approves of her; his behaviour puzzles me.

If Sarah had been able to hear Julian's words and follow his actions over the next hour or so, she would have found the answer to why he had behaved to Crystal de Florette as he had done. And she would have been reassured.

As Julian Cleeve handed Crystal up into his carriage, he was thinking furiously. I have got her out of the house, but that is not enough. She will not do for Lord Hadlow, anyone can see that. I believe I am right in thinking that she imagines to marry a baron is to marry money; and it is quite obvious that she thinks that James is the owner of Cleeve Grange. Silly boy, yet he is a nicely mannered young man and quite handsome.

But I must say something to Miss Florette and it is a very short drive to the Grange. He sat beside her and felt dwarfed by the ridiculous coiffure and the tall plumes of her head-dress.

'Miss Florette,' he began in a pleasant manner. 'I am pleased to welcome you to Cleeve Grange. It is my family home, you know, and I am very proud of it. You have known James long?'

He could hear a falter in her reply. 'Oh yes, we met a month ago just as he was celebrating his degree . . . but, Mr Cleeve, you say that Cleeve Grange is in your family? I understood James to say he had grown up there and that you were here on a visit.'

'He did grow up there, that is quite correct. Lord Hadlow – his father, that is – rented the Grange from my father. It was when my father went to America and Lord Hadlow had to sell out and was glad to find a good place at a reasonable rent.'

'Rent?' the actress echoed and her voice became feeble. 'I had thought that James owned the estate.'

'No, you are mistaken. I am the owner and I have rather wickedly turned the family out and they are forced to make shift with Little Cleeve; a nice house but rather cramped and only four bedrooms. But they seem comfortable there, I must say. I am sorry that they did not have a room for you, but I can assure you that you are very welcome at Cleeve Grange. No trouble at all. And Anita and Marianne will be pleased to have you. Anita is glad to settle in England; it is not just a visit, we have decided to make our home here.'

'But. . . .'

'Here we are, let me help you down and introduce you to Mrs Stockdale, my housekeeper. She always keeps the best guest room ready for a visitor.'

They walked up the steps of the Grange and Julian was thinking, so far so good; I have sown the seeds of doubt in her mind. She is a money grabber, I am certain of it.

Miss Florette was greeted by a cheerful Mrs Stockdale who was told the news of the betrothal. She obviously did her best to mask her surprise at Mr Cleeve's guest. That the painted actress could be the betrothed of Lord Hadlow had given the housekeeper a shock and it showed in her face.

But her words were kind and she took Crystal up to the guest room where she arranged to have a fire lit.

Downstairs, Julian waited in the drawing-room. I do not know James, he was saying to himself, only what Sarah has told me of him. He has stuck to his studies which is to his credit, and from what he says, he has obtained a diplomatic post. He has done well, but he genuinely seems to believe that I am here on a visit and that the Grange will revert to him eventually.

But the actress? Crystal de Florette indeed! She might be beautiful in James's eyes, but without the paint she would look almost as old as his mother. Crystal believes him to be wealthy and for some reason known only to himself, he has let her be misinformed. But he is young and will come about; it is up to me to get rid of the lady – if I can call her a lady. A strumpet would be nearer the mark, he told himself grimly.

When his guest rejoined him in the drawing-room, even Julian was shocked and he considered himself to be used to the ways of the world. She had removed her travelling coat and her headdress, but her fair hair was still piled high. She had renewed the rouge on her cheeks and lips and had placed a patch on the corner of her mouth.

As if that was not enough, Crystal was wearing one of the most daring and revealing dresses he had ever seen; it was of a fine muslin of a vivid pink and she had dampened her chemise so that the diaphanous gown clung to her voluptuous body. In style it was fashionable for it had a high waist, tiny puffed sleeves and a tight-fitting bodice. It was the bodice that riveted Julian's attention for the thin fabric was cut so low and the waist pushed up so high, that it appeared almost as though her ample breasts would burst out of the gown's confines.

She cannot be seen in front of Lady Hadlow or Bertram dressed like that, Julian vowed. I am sure now of what I must do. And I know that Sarah would wish me to do it even though she must be thinking that I made Miss Florette more than welcome in bringing her here to Cleeve Grange.

'Come and sit down, my dear,' he said. 'You look charming, the colour suits.'

She was holding a gilded fan and fluttered ostentatiously. 'Oh la, Mr Cleeve, I purchased this gown especially to please James. Do you think he will like it?'

'Without a doubt,' replied Julian, still glib in manner. 'I am sure he will be along soon when he has spoken to Lady Hadlow, and then I must take the carriage back to fetch Anita and Marianne.'

'Marianne is James's younger sister?' she asked. 'I remember him telling me that he had an older sister and another one younger than himself. She is a pretty girl and so is your daughter.'

'Yes,' agreed Julian smoothly and then made the plunge. 'The Wintersons were in a sad state when I arrived. They had spent their last penny in sending James to Oxford and Lady Hadlow could not afford to give poor litttle Marianne a season. So I invited her here to be a companion to my Anita and I am going to launch both of them into the ton later this month. I hope you will still be here. . . .'

But he knew he had lost the actress's attention. Her expression was a mixture of alarm, greediness and a certain bewilderment.

'Mr Cleeve, are you telling me that James has no money? I don't think I can believe you, indeed I can't. I always wanted to marry a lord but I thought I would have to settle for one of those fat old gentlemen who slaver all over you. When I met James – it was after the performance, you know – and he told me he was a baron I was sure he had been sent by the gods. I'm not saying that I wanted to marry him just because of that for I do love him, just as he loves me. Proper little love birds, we are, the two of us. But I would like to know where I stand . . . as far as the money is concerned, that is,' she added hastily.

Julian took his opportunity and knew he was doing it slyly. 'James has little fortune,' he told her. 'Scarcely more than an independence; but you need not worry, Miss Florette, he will command a salary from the Foreign Office and he has a good career in front of him. I am certain that he is able as well as intelligent.'

'You mean, Mr Cleeve, that James will only have his salary and could be posted anywhere in the world?'

Julian nearly laughed at the woebegone question. 'That is so, it will be a splendid life.'

'La, yes, so it will. I never expected to be an ambassador's wife, after all.'

'No, I do not suppose you did.' Thinking he had said enough for the time being, Julian got up. 'Now I am going to leave you while I take the carriage back to Little Cleeve for Anita and Marianne. I am sure that James will be here any minute so you will not be on your own. There are some fashion books of Anita's that you might like to look at. They are on the small table by the window.

'Thank you, Mr Cleeve, you are very kind, I must say.'

Julian let himself out of the house and hurried round to the stables where the carriage was waiting. Have I succeeded in putting her off the idea of a marriage to James, he was asking himself? Will she be there when I get back?

Six

BY THIS TIME Julian had the freedom of coming and going at Little Cleeve without the formality and bother of being admitted and shown out by the Wintersons' only maid.

That day, he jumped from the carriage, opened the front door and in the entrance hall, was met by a whirlwind of a Sarah. She had been on the listen for his arrival and wanted very much to speak to him privately before he entered the drawing-room.

Julian took one look at Sarah's face and caught hold of her arms before she had the chance to strike him as she had nearly done once before.

'Julian, why did you do it? We could all see what a dreadful creature James had with him, but we were lost for words. Philip was not here to help and Bertram had his hands full tending to Mama. I relied on you. But what did you do? I could not believe my ears when you made her so welcome; and then to make her a guest at Cleeve Grange. It is beyond any understanding. Why, Julian, why. . . .?'

Holding her arms he pulled her towards him, looking down at her enraged face with a smile. 'You do not trust me, Cousin,' he said.

Her eyes blazed. 'Of course I do not trust you even if I have said I would marry you. How can I? "May I congratulate you and welcome you to the family". Those were your very words to her and you could see as well as I could that she was a painted Jezebel of a woman. My poor mother is distracted and as for James, all he will say is that he and Crystal love one another and he is certain that she will make him a good wife. She is a very clever actress, he keeps saying. What shall we do? Oh, Julian, do tell me that you did not mean to like her so whole-heartedly. She is not respectable, you know. I do not know whether to be angry with you, or to try and plead our cause.' She broke off as he started to walk away. 'What are you doing?'

He was leading her to a long, low wooden stool at the foot of the staircase. 'Sit down and listen to me. Give me your hands and try and believe that I am sincere. Can you do that?'

She sighed as she sat down. 'I will try.'

'I saw as well as you did that Crystal de Florette was nothing but a trollop—'

'Julian,' she protested.

'You want the truth, do you not? I liked the look of young James; but your mother was immediately prostrated – it was a good thing that she had Bertram at her side. You looked as though you had been struck dumb.'

'It is an accurate description,' she said bitterly. 'So what did you do but welcome her with open arms.'

'Be quiet.'

'It is not easy.'

'Well, you will have to try or we will have the family coming out to see what we are up to. What are they doing, by the way?' he asked.

'Bertram has gone back to Luttons Park and James is seated with Mama in charge of the vinaigrette and hartshorn, and Marianne and Anita have got a fit of the giggles at the thought of having someone like Crystal de Florette as a relative.'

'Little monkeys. Listen. I always seem to be telling you to listen to me. I had to do something about the actress, so I spoke nicely to her and carried her off to Cleeve Grange.' He stopped and gave a sudden laugh.

'Whatever is funny in the situation?'

'You should see her! She has changed into a very low-cut clinging gown which would shock even the most libertine of the undergraduates at Oxford. It shocked me and that is saying something. I wonder what James will think?'

'Please go on with your purpose,' she replied stonily.

'She had thought that the Grange belonged to James, I soon disillusioned her about that. I have also hinted that he has no money and a family to provide for. She does not like that either and I left her thinking it over.' He put his hands gently on her shoulders. 'Leave it all to me, my sweet. I promise you that Miss Crystal de Florette will be out of the district within twenty-four hours and that James's heart will not be broken.'

She gazed into his eyes, saw that he was serious and gave a sigh of relief. 'Thank you, Julian. I do trust you and I am sorry I was angry with you.'

He dropped a light kiss on her cheek. 'Good girl, now let us go and see your mama.'

Sarah thought that James looked relieved to see Julian. He got up immediately. 'Good of you to take Crystal to the Grange, Cousin. May I walk over and see her now?'

'Yes, of course; she is changed and waiting for you. I told her you would soon be with her.' Julian put a hand on the young man's arm. 'A minute though, James. Why have you let Miss Florette think that you owned Cleeve Grange and the estate?'

James flushed, but he looked his cousin straight in the eye and spoke in an outright manner. 'A stupid mistake owing to Mama's appalling handwriting. She has explained it to me now. I had thought you to be making a visit to this country with Anita and wanted to be at the Grange for a few weeks. I had imagined that when you returned to America, it would be ours again. I know that it is only rented from you, but I have never known any other home. We have kept it looking nice, too.' He paused and then spoke very hurriedly. 'Crystal will understand; I expect to be out of the country on some diplomatic mission in any case.'

Sarah saw Julian give one of his charming smiles and she could not believe the wicked insincerity of his words. 'Off you go and explain it to the young lady and I wish you joy.'

James kissed his mother and made his farewells and as soon as he was out of the house, Julian took his seat at Lady Hadlow's side.

She put out a quivering hand. 'Such a shock, Cousin. What is James thinking of, bringing such a creature to my house and saying that she is going to be his wife? I thought I should swoon when I saw her, dressed like a harlot and her face painted as though she was still on the stage. I have talked to James but he cannot see it. Whatever shall we do?'

Julian took the feeble hand in his firm grasp. 'My dear Cousin Mary, do not fret for I have it all in hand. I do not think you are going to have to go through the worry of having to accept Miss Crystal de Florette as a daughter-in-law.'

'You are so good, Julian. I am afraid that dear Bertram was very shocked; I do hope that he doesn't cry off for I love him dearly and will be very happy at Luttons Park with him.'

'Have no fear, Cousin. I have made a promise to Sarah that Miss Florette will be out of the district by tomorrow and I repeat it to you. So pluck up. James will soon make a recover and he can go round the estate with me if he wishes to.'

'You are all kindness, Julian,' replied Lady Hadlow.

Julian turned to the young people who had been listening enthralled. 'Come along, you two moppets, we'll have another turn at teaching me to play Speculation to give young James a chance to visit his beloved, and then I will take you home.'

James had decided to ride rather than walk to the Grange and although he was not wearing riding clothes, he found Reuben, saddled his own horse, Turk, and was soon at the big house. He was feeling confused.

The weeks he had spent in Crystal's company after taking his finals had been sweet indeed; he had accepted that she was an actress, but she was so pretty and nicely behaved. And she had showered him with so much flattery, he had thought her a pearl. Now, seeing her in his own home and amongst his family, he was assailed with doubts especially at his mother's hysterical reaction.

He was feeling neither happy nor confident as he left Turk at the stables and let himself in the front door of the Grange; he guessed that he would find Crystal in the drawing-room.

Meeting the housekeeper on the way in, he greeted her cheerfully. 'Hallo, you must be Mrs Stockdale, I am Hadlow.'

'Pleased to meet you My Lord, I'm sure. Miss Florette is in the drawing-room and I think she is expecting you.'

James, standing in the doorway of the drawing-room, was confronted with a discontented woman he hardly recognized.

Crystal came towards him with a frown and he was struck, not only by her vulgarity which he thought must have been evident to his family, but by the unsuitability of the gown she was wearing. Her exposed breasts were heaving with indignation and he was so shocked, he did not know whether he should shower her soft flesh with kisses as he would have done a week ago, or to cover her with the flimsy shawl which was draped round her arms.

'James, my sweet boy, what have you been telling me? I thought that Cleeve Grange was your country seat and now I discover that it belongs to your handsome American cousin. Is he not dashing? And so polite and kind, too. Bringing me here and giving me a sumptuous bedroom – Mrs Stockdale has even had a fire lit for me though I can tell she does not approve of me. And then your cousin told me how charming I looked in this new gown of mine which I had made especially to please you and to wear in the country. I am not used to country ways, as you know, and I thought I must do my best and not put dear James to shame. Tell me, do you admire my gown?'

James, who thought she looked like no female he had ever seen before except in the bawdy prints of Rowlandson which had circulated at the university, was lost for words.

'It is very nice, Crystal, but is it not rather low in the bodice?' he added.

She laughed with a harsh parody of a laugh which mocked his modest manner. 'Oh la, I do believe Lord Hadlow is a prude and does not approve of the latest fashion when he sees it. Bang up to the nines it is, as you gentleman would say. I think your cousin liked it for he could not take his eyes off me. Now tell me about him, James, is he wealthy?'

James shifted uncomfortably but had sat down at her side on the sofa where she immediately moved her thigh close to his and put an arm around his neck.

'I do not know a lot about my cousin,' he began. 'I had misled you about the Grange because I thought he was here on a short visit, I am sorry, Crystal. His father was supposed to have made a fortune in America, but what has passed on to Julian, I have no way of knowing.'

'I shall have to find out.'

'What do you mean?' He put out a hand to the scandalous bodice of the gown and she quickly knocked it away.

'No, none of those tricks, we are talking business.'

'Are we?'

'Yes, you know very well I wanted to marry an earl or baron, at the least. Well, you are Lord Hadlow, but what is the use of that if you have neither estate nor fortune? Have you an income, James?'

'I have no fortune certainly, but I will have a good salary once

I am in the Foreign Office. We should be able to marry, Crystal, and money is not everything. We do love each other.'

'Bah, what is love without money? I am disappointed in you, James, but you can give me a kiss if you like.'

James stood up. 'I do not want to kiss you in this mood,' he said stiffly. 'I will let you settle into Cleeve Grange and come and see you in the morning.'

'Very well, it suits me for I will be able to find out the extent of your cousin's fortune by this evening.'

James flung out of the house in a state of disgust and disillusionment. He rode home to Little Cleeve not noticing that he passed the Cleeve carriage on its way back to the Grange.

Inside the carriage, Julian was talking earnestly to Anita and Marianne. 'There is not a lot of time and I must impress on you that Miss Crystal de Florette will not do for James. You do understand, do you not?'

'She is shockingly vulgar, Papa,' said Anita with a giggle. 'But there was something jolly about her, I cannot say that I disliked her.'

'That is well said, Anita,' her father replied. 'For I want you to be very friendly towards Miss Florette after dinner this evening when the tea-tray is brought in. Impress on her that I am a man of great wealth, that you are an heiress, anything like that.'

Anita was wide-eyed. 'You are not going to steal her from James, are you, Papa? But of course, you are now betrothed to Sarah, which is very nice.'

Julian laughed. 'No, Anita, do not fear, the likes of Crystal de Florette will not replace Sarah in my affections. I simply want to break up the association between James and the actress.'

Marianne spoke for the first time. 'But, Cousin Julian, I think James will see it for himself now that he has brought her home to meet us. I do believe you could safely leave it to him, he usually has great sense.'

'He showed little sense in becoming involved with someone like Miss Florette,' he said to her.

But Anita was laughing merrily. 'That was no more than a university prank,' she said. 'Boys will be boys.'

Julian looked at her. 'You are old beyond your years and I did not realize it, Anita.'

'It comes of living solely in your company, Papa.'

'Minx, I do not know how I allow such impertinence.'

'You love me, Papa,' the young girl said and reached up to kiss him and by that time, they had arrived at the Grange.

When the two girls were dressed ready for dinner and waiting to go downstairs. Marianne asked Anita what she thought of James's affair with Crystal de Florette.

Anita was her usual candid self. 'I think I would like to know James better when he has forgotten about Crystal. I am certain that Papa will have her out of the way before tomorrow is out, he loves to order other people's lives and we know what he thinks about Crystal.'

Marianne smiled. 'He managed to secure Sarah for himself and I know you are pleased about that. And now Mama is going to marry Bertram which is the best thing which could have happened.'

'He will be finding someone for you next, Marianne.'

'You are a romantic, Anita, I do believe.'

'Well, are you not a romantic, as well?' Anita asked.

'I suppose I could be but I have never met any gentleman to be romantic about; the only gentlemen I know are Sir Bertram and Cousin Julian and they are ancient!'

Anita was thoughtful. 'What about Philip?'

Marianne frowned. 'Do you know, I always thought Sarah would marry Philip once he had forgotten about his Clara, but it was Bertram who offered for her.'

'There is always Jane Humphries' older brother, Oliver; he is not married yet.'

'You are trying to match-make,' laughed Marianne. 'In any case, Oliver has just become betrothed to a young lady called Hester Brewer for Jane told me so. He met her in London and Jane does not like her.'

'Perhaps we could tell Papa and he will do something about it,' said Anita.

'Oh, Anita, what will you say next, you are a complete case. I think it is time to go down for dinner. Do not forget what your papa wished you to say to Miss Florette,' Marianne reminded her.

'No, I have not forgotten. Be careful, just listen to me and do not interrupt if I shock you.'

And after dinner, Marianne listened in fascination. Crystal had changed into a more formal gown so that the sensibilities of the two girls were not offended. They sat over the tea~tray and Anita began her little scene.

'I do admire my Cousin James, Miss Florette. 1 had not met him until today, you know. You will like being Lady Hadlow?'

Crystal looked from one girl to the other thinking that they looked like young innocents and lived in a very protected world.

'I will be honest, Miss Anita, and tell you that I have had a sad disappointment today. Two disappointments, in fact.'

'Oh, Miss Florette, I am sorry, do you wish to tell us about it? Is there any way in which we could help you?'

'No, bless your hearts, and do please call me by my name. I am Crystal to all my friends. And Florette is not my proper name after all, I made it up for the stage. I was born Martha Suggitt, but I didn't think that was in the least suitable for an actress.'

'Have you been an actress for very long, Crystal?' asked Anita in a friendly manner.

'Oh la, yes I have, for my ma put me into pantaloons and made me play the boy when I was only ten years old. And that was over twenty years ago. Oh, there I go, my silly tongue. I have let you know my age is over thirty and even James don't know that. He thinks I am just twenty.'

'I am sure you look no more then eighteen, Crystal,' announced Anita with great gusto and accompanied by a giggle from Marianne. 'That is just the same age as Marianne and me.'

'It is kind of you to say, I'm sure, Miss Anita. There are times when I feel my real age. It was lovely when I met James. But now it has all gone wrong.'

'You were going to tell us about your troubles, Crystal.'

'I don't know as I should but you see I had set my heart on marrying a lord with a big estate and a fortune. And when James came along and he was so young and handsome, I thought "Crystal, this is it". I really did, that's what I thought. And I come here and I dress myself so grand so you would like me, you've no idea how much those plumes cost me. But now I've found him out. It's your papa as owns the Grange, Miss Anita, and I believe James hasn't a penny to bless himself with.'

At these words, Anita came out with her set piece and Marianne was proud of her. 'No, the Wintersons are quite poor. My papa lets them have Little Cleeve rent free, you know. He is the one with the fortune, but he is not a lord anything, so he would not do for you, Crystal. In any case he has just become betrothed to Marianne's sister. I am a considerable heiress, but that does not help you either. Papa says that when I make my come-out, I will have all the gazetted fortune-hunters after me. He even said that they will come flocking out of London to Tunbridge Wells when they hear of my fortune, but I think he was only saying it for fun just to tease me. He will watch me very carefully, I do believe.'

Marianne noticed that there was a glimmer in Crystal's eyes that had not been there before; then the actress tried not to sound too eager as she spoke to Anita.

'La, Miss Anita, you are a lucky girl. But I don't suppose an

American fortune is anything like as great as some of our English dukes and earls.'

Anita gave a short laugh and Marianne thought there was a wickedness hidden in her voice. 'Oh no, you are quite wrong, Crystal; you have no idea of the fortunes to be made on the tobacco plantations of Virginia. Papa says he could buy Carlton House if he wanted to.'

'Buy Carlton House?' Crystal's voice was a screech of amazement. 'But that's the Regent's London house and they say it is the grandest mansion in the land. You cannot be serious, Miss Anita.'

'My papa would not tell me anything that was not true,' said Anita solemnly and then got up. 'Now I think I am tired. Shall we go up to our rooms, Marianne? We will see you in the morning, Crystal. It has been nice talking to you.'

They left a thoughtful Crystal downstairs and went in search of Anita's father to say goodnight. He, too, was sitting thoughtfully, but in the library with an untouched glass of port in front of him.

'Goodnight, my rascals,' he said and gave each of them a kiss. 'Have you succeeded in what I asked you to do, Anita? . . . oh, I can see by the mischief on your face that you have. I will see you in the morning.'

In Anita's bedroom – Marianne had a smaller room next to it – the two girls collapsed on to the bed laughing.

'Anita, you are wicked and you should not have said that about Carlton House. I am sure Cousin Julian never told you such a thing.'

'No, I was making it up, but he would not mind; it is true that he always tells me the truth. I know that he would think that I was just romancing over Carlton House. It sounded very grand, did it not?'

'You are a quiz, Anita,' laughed Marianne. 'I love being with you for I never know what you are going to say next. I wonder what will happen tomorrow?'

The first thing that happened the next day was that Miss Crystal de Florette rose betimes and went downstairs for an early breakfast. She found Julian Cleeve already at the table which was just what she had hoped for . . . indeed, had planned.

Her dress that morning was of a vivid red and white striped sarsenet, it had a high neck and she wore it with a string of what passed for bright green emeralds which hung almost to her waist. She also wore the jewels in her hair and knew that it looked quite vulgar and most unsuitable for a morning stay in a country house. But she had laid her plans.

'Good morning, Mr Cleeve,' she said politely, as she sat opposite to him.

Julian was prepared for anything, even the red and white stripes. 'Good morning, Crystal. And do please call me Julian, I would like that.'

'Certainly, Julian, I would like to know you better for I have something to discuss with you.'

'I expect you have,' he answered drily.

She put some butter on a wafer-thin slice of toast and bit daintily into it, managing to look very innocent at the same time. Miss Florette was not an actress for nothing.

'I am afraid I have upset James and I had no wish to do that, indeed I didn't, for I am very fond of him. I will be quite honest and tell you that it came as a great shock to me to discover that although he is Lord Hadlow, he is a gentleman of no fortune. Not a sixpence to scratch with, as they say. And you are the owner of this lovely house, Julian, I had not expected that. I had thought it would all be mine one day.' She paused and looked at her host over the top of her tea cup. She was satisfied that she had his attention.

'But I have lain awake nearly all night thinking of dear James,' she continued. 'He is quite the one for me, 1 am sure of that. And I must tell you, Julian, that I have made my decision.'

'You have, Crystal?' Julian was prepared for all this, but even he had underestimated the wiles of Miss Florette.

'Yes. What is money, I have asked myself. It is love that is of the first importance; I kept saying it time and time again. And I do love James, there is no denying it. Quite a novel sensation for me for I've known many gentlemen, lords included, as you may well guess. So, I thought in the end, I am going to have my James, money or no money. I will make sure he will get into diplomatic circles in London, he doesn't need to be posted abroad. He will be Lord Hadlow at the Foreign Office and, of course, I will be Lady Hadlow and proud of it. And with his salary, we will rent a little house and we can come down into Kent so that he can see his family. There, I have it all worked out; I think James will be pleased, don't you?'

Julian was thinking fast. She is clever, there is no denying it. It is blackmail and she knows very well that I can and will pay handsomely to get her out of the way. I will not beat about the bush.

'How much, Miss Florette?' he said bluntly.

'How much do I love James, do you mean? Oh, I love him more than I can say. No money in the world can make me give him up.'

'How much, Miss Florette?' Julian repeated grimly.

'Whatever are you saying, Julian? I don't understand you.'

'You understand me very well. You are a vulgar strumpet and you do not stop short at blackmail. It is probably not the first time that you have acted your way through an escapade of this sort. How much money do you want me to give you in order to keep you away from Lord Hadlow?'

The actress knew she had won and she let the pose drop. 'You're not short of a penny or two and won't find it hard to raise the wind, I know that. I might have been deceived in James but I know that you're well-to-do in the world for Miss Anita told me so. I'll settle for a thousand.'

Even Julian was shocked, but he did not show it. 'It will be half of that and not a penny more,' he said.

Crystal got up, not concealing the glint of triumph in her eyes. 'Very well, I'll settle for five hundred guineas and you'll take me up to London before James has time to come calling.'

'I'll give you ten minutes to pack your bags.' Julian rose and walked to the door.

'They're packed.'

'Doxy,' he returned coolly, and went to get his travelling cape and bag and to order the carriage. Then to tell Anita what was happening.

Anita and Marianne, in fact, were at that moment coming down the stairs for breakfast.

'Anita, there you are,' said her father. 'I am taking Miss Florette back to London immediately. I may be gone a few days as I have some business to see to.'

Anita's grin could only be described as pert. 'How much did it cost you, Papa?' she asked him.

'Anita,' Julian Cleeve was shocked for the second time in the space of a few minutes. 'You will have to learn some propriety. American manners will not do here.'

Anita gave him a kiss. 'You are the perfect gentleman. We will go and say goodbye to Crystal.'

Miss Florette was in fact about to leave the breakfast-room, very pleased with herself and eager to be gone.

'Miss Anita?' she said, for the first time at a loss.

'Goodbye, Miss Florette,' said Anita with great poise as she took in the red stripes and the enormous loop of green stones. 'Do have a good journey. I do admire the dress you are wearing.'

'Goodbye,' muttered the actress and fled.

Marianne looked at Anita. 'You are a rogue,' she said. 'You look so small and harmless and yet you have a wicked wit.'

And they both laughed at the incident of Miss Crystal de Florette all the way through breakfast and for most of the day.

Seven

ANITA AND MARIANNE, having partaken of their breakfast, were deciding what to do with the morning when James arrived.

He had ridden over on Turk and looked his best in riding breeches and nicely cut coat; but his temper was uncertain. He stood in the drawing-room and looked at the two girls.

'Where is Crystal?' he asked them, and Anita thought she could sense a slight edge to his voice.

'Gone,' she replied.

He looked then at his young sister. 'Has Anita got windmills in her head? Where is Crystal, Marianne?'

Marianne loved her brother and knew that she would be too gentle with him and soon put him out of temper. She decided that the newly sharp Anita would deal with him better.

'Anita is telling you the truth,' she replied. 'Let her tell you about it.'

'I don't want to talk to Anita, I want to talk to Crystal. I have something important to say to her.' James walked across the room to where Anita was sitting on the sofa; he stood looking down at her. She had a mischievous look in her eyes as he sat at her side and she turned to face him. 'Now what is all this nonsense?' he asked rather tetchily. 'I will start again. Please will you tell me where Crystal is for it is imperative that I see her immediately.'

Thinking that he was going to be upset that Crystal had gone, Anita put out a hand and placed it on his. James did not take his hand away and continued to look at her.

'Well, Anita?'

'James, it is true that Crystal has gone. Papa has taken her back to London in the carriage.'

'You mean that she is not coming back again?' James's voice was unsure.

'No, she is not coming back. I believe she had discovered that you were on the rocks and that Papa was wealthy and somehow I think she blackmailed him into giving her money. He did not consider that she was suitable, you know . . . James.' Anita gave a cry for James had taken her by the hands, pulled her off the sofa and whirled her round.

'Hurrah,' James shouted, and there was both triumph and relief in his voice. 'What a let out. I could kiss you, Anita.'

'I don't mind.'

And James bent forward and dropped the lightest of kisses on her lips which surprised Anita as much as it surprised James.

'Marianne, too,' James said, and turned and kissed his sister. 'I think the two of you have been in this together.'

Anita was clinging on to his hands and looking at him with astonishment. 'James, do you mean that you do not mind?'

He laughed then. And the three of them sat on the sofa and talked and laughed together.

'I have been a fool,' he told them. 'A block, mutton-headed, whatever you like to call it. I thought I had made a tremendous conquest. Crystal was much sought after in Oxford, but as soon as I brought her home here, I realized that I was making a dreadful mistake. Mama had the vapours, you all looked stony-faced, only Cousin Julian had the wit to do something about it. I must thank him the minute he gets back.' He looked at the two faces. 'You really do mean it? I was going to have to tell Crystal that I could not marry her and I was afraid that she would demand money, or bring a breach of promise or something like that. My pockets are to let . . . dammit, if Cousin Julian has paid her to go back to London then I suppose I am in his debt.' He gave a frown.

Anita touched his arm. 'Do not worry, James, Papa is as rich as a nabob and will not even notice it. In any case, he will tell you that he is already in debt to you for letting Marianne come and live with me. I was a timid little thing before she came . . . with my limp and everything.'

James looked at her. 'You timid, Anita? I do not believe a word of it. And you don't limp, do you? I've not noticed.'

'Yes, I do. I was unseated when we lived in America and I broke my leg. It did not mend properly and I have limped ever since. I have never ridden again either.'

'Never ridden again? Do you mean that you are frightened of being on horseback?'

'Yes, I shall never get on a horse again, I feel sure,' replied Anita.

But James would not have it. 'Nonsense, I will get you up on a horse, you wait and see. I will have you galloping around the estate in no time.'

Anita laughed. 'Papa would willingly excuse you the debt if you did that, James. You will have to speak to him when he returns from London.'

'I will do,' he said, and he left them to go and carry his news to Sarah and Lady Hadlow.

His words to his mother almost produced another fit of the vapours, but this time, it was because of her tremendous relief and delight.

Sarah voiced the thoughts of both of them. 'James, you gave us a fright producing an actress as your future wife, but I am pleased you have seen sense so quickly.'

He grinned ruefully. 'It did not take me long to realize how unsuitable she was and then I soon discovered that she had little interest in me when she found out there was no money. I think we have our cousin to thank for all that.'

Sarah agreed. 'Yes, I will go over and thank him when he returns from London.'

'He is to be gone for a few days, Anita told me,' James said to her. 'And when he comes home, I am going to offer to get Anita riding again. I cannot offer to reimburse him for whatever he had to pay Crystal, but at least I am certain that I could persuade Anita on to a horse again.' He looked at his sister and his mother and could not help but notice that they seemed a little easier. 'I am feeling rather unsettled after this business, Sarah; I think I will ride over to see Philip. He always talks good sense to me.'

'I wish he would to me,' replied Sarah enigmatically, but James had gone.

There was little more than six years difference in age between Philip and James, but when James had been a boy, he had hero-worshipped the older Philip. Once James had gone to Oxford, they remained good friends and he knew he was always welcome at the dower house at Luttons Park.

James rode Turk at full stretch and was glad to feel the air rush past him, to see the full green of the summer woods and fields, and to hear the reassuring thud of hooves on the turf.

He had not expected to find Philip in as it was mid-morning, but he was made welcome by Mrs Bainbridge.

'Master James,' she beamed, they were all still boys to the good housekeeper. 'Mr Philip's over at Stoddarts. Why don't you go and meet him and I'll have a nuncheon for the two of you when you come back.'

James knew the Luttons estate as thoroughly as he knew Cleeve and was pleased to ride to Stoddarts farm which took him up to Covert Wood and then down the bridle-way to the farm. It was here that he met Philip who was on his way home.

'James, I heard you were home,' was Philip's cheery greeting. 'What the devil's all this about you bringing an actress with you?'

James groaned. 'I've disgraced the family, Philip, can I come and talk to you? Mrs Bainbridge is going to have a nuncheon ready for us, I called at the dower house first.'

Philip grinned. 'We can share our woes over some small beer. I'm not very pleased with myself either.'

Ten minutes later, they were sitting on the settle in the breakfast room with a plate of ham and pickles and their tankards full of the ale brewed at Luttons Park.

'I've been a regular dolt, a chuckle-head, Philip: you would never think I had just been three years at Oxford studying for the law. I think it must have injured my brain for I fell in love with an actress – I cannot bear to tell you the whole. But I thought she was the last thing in beauty until I got her home and heard her talking to Mama in the drawing-room. Poor Mama, if it hadn't been for Bertram, I think she would have had hysterics. And what is all this about Mama and Bertram? I thought Bertram was set on having Sarah for his wife.'

Philip looked glum. 'I'll tell you in a minute. But have you got rid of the actress? And how did you do it?'

'It was our new cousin, she blackmailed him and he has taken her off to London. Now I feel that I should repay him, but I am run off my legs – all to pieces. So when he returns from London, I am hoping to bargain with him over Anita.'

Philip was bewildered. 'Anita? Where does she come into it? And before you go any further, I must tell you that your Cousin Julian is not in favour with me.'

'Why is that?' James gave a slight frown. 'He seems to me to be a capital fellow and just right for Sarah though I have a feeling that she doesn't love him. Still, I expect it will serve. What have you got against him?'

'He has stolen Sarah from me, that is all,' Philip said gloomily.

It was James's turn to look bewildered. 'But, Philip, you have always led us to believe that you would never marry again. Did you ask Sarah to be your wife and she turned down the offer?'

'I did ask her, but I only said it jokingly and she went off and accepted Julian Cleeve. I'm jealous. I never in my life thought I would be capable of plain jealousy, but as soon as I saw them together and they made their announcement, I went into a blind rage and took it out on Sarah. I am afraid that I did not behave very well and I don't think she will ever turn to me again. We have always been such friends.'

'Do you love her?' James asked bluntly.

Philip thought before he replied. 'The thing is I don't know. I loved Clara so very much, but we were young and I've always thought I would never love anyone else. But how I feel for Sarah is competely different, I hardly understand it and I cannot explain it. In any case, it is no good because she has engaged herself to marry Cleeve.'

James spoke slowly. 'Do you know, Philip, I have a feeling that Julian asked her simply to stop her marrying Bertram. We always said it would not do, remember? And now Bertram has turned to Mama and it is comic to see them together. But I must not laugh, he is your brother. What do you make of it all?'

'I am pleased for them both. Lady Hadlow has lost Cleeve Grange and I think she is very suited to be mistress of Luttons Park. But you realize something, James?'

'What is that?'

'It means that Bertram will not have an heir and I am the only other son, so it is up to me to be married and produce a Hesslewood heir.'

'Good God, I never thought of that. Sarah would have been just right for you.'

Philip managed a grin. 'Don't rub it in.'

'What about Marianne?'

Philip looked startled. 'Marianne? Damme, I never thought of that. I still think of her as a schoolroom miss.'

'She is a very pretty girl,' said James rather amused. 'She is sharing a come-out ball with Anita and Jane Humphries. Do you know the Humphries? They live in a big house in Tunbridge Wells.'

'I don't know them well, though I do recall that there was a son just a bit younger than me, Oliver I think his name is. Decent young man, was up at Oxford and then became a lawyer in London. But what has this to do with things?'

'I think the plan is for us all to go there for dinner very soon to make the arrangements for the come-out ball. You would be able to talk to Marianne then. I don't suppose you have seen a lot of her since she went to the Grange as Anita's companion.'

'Not trying to get me fixed up, by any chance, young James? Now that I have been foolish enough to lose Sarah.'

James was pleased to hear Philip talking more in his usual light-hearted way. 'I don't think I would be a very good match-maker,' he replied in the same vein. 'Leave it to the old tabbies at the ball. And after that we go to Brighton for August. Will you be going with us?'

Philip nodded. 'For a few days, at least. There is too much for me to do here for me to be away for very long. It is Bertram's greatest moment of the year, meeting up with the Regent again. And what are you going to do with yourself until then? I had better try and keep you out of mischief! Don't fancy coming over here and helping me, do you? It is a busy time of year with the harvest coming up.'

James felt a rush of relief at the thought of escaping from his mother and his sisters. He loved them dearly but they would be forever reminding him of his foolishness over Crystal.

'I would like it very much, Philip, I accept gladly. I have only one commitment in the next few weeks and that is to persuade Anita to start riding again . . . why do you look like that?' James noticed a deep frown on his friend's face.

Philip got up and walked to the window which looked out over the fields of Luttons Park. 'I am not sure, James, and it is something that contributed to my quarrel with Sarah. I had better not mention it again.'

'You can tell me, surely.'

'I thought there was something not quite the gentleman about your cousin right from the start. It may be because he is American and not used to our English ways, I don't know. Sarah just laughed at me. And it is not just your cousin, it is Anita as well.'

James joined him at the window. 'Whatever can you mean? She is only little and I think she is quite pretty. Not that I am interested. I've done with the petticoat line for a while until I get myself established at the Foreign Office. But the little I have seen of Anita gave me the impression that she was a lively little girl, outspoken, too. Do you know her well?'

'I hardly know her at all. It is not a question of how well I know her and no doubt this is going to sound foolish. She has a pronounced limp and she says she is afraid of horses since her accident, but I swear I have seen her and her father out riding together early in the morning. Anywhere between here and Cleeve Grange. Sarah thought I was mistaken.'

It was James's turn to frown. 'I think you must have been, Philip. I have just been talking to her about it. I hope to get her riding again and I am going to promise it to my cousin in return for his help in getting rid of Crystal.'

Philip gave a rueful grin. 'You can prove me wrong. I will ask you again in a few days' time. Enough of the American visitors, let us go and tell Mrs Bainbridge to prepare a room for you and then we'll get Reuben to bring everything you need in the carriage. I am off to the top farm now and will see you later.'

James sought out Sarah as soon as he returned to Little Cleeve and they walked in the garden together.

'Sarah, I have been to see Philip. He is regretting he did not offer for you before Julian did! But I sincerely wish you happiness with our cousin. I must say he succeeded in getting me out of a hole. I am sorry about Crystal, Sarah, I must have taken leave of my senses, bringing her here like that.'

Sarah smiled. He had always been the 'little brother' and she loved him and felt protective towards him in the same way as she did towards Marianne.

'I will be honest with you, James: I am more than fond of Philip, but the ghost of Clara always seems to be present. Poor Clara. If I do not love Julian in quite the same way, it amounts to very little, for it is a match that is advantageous to us as a family. . . .'

'Oh, Sarah, don't do it for us,' James interrupted. 'We cannot expect it of you. You have borne the brunt of Father's misdemeanours all these years and now the time has come for you to be happy.'

Sarah smiled at his earnestness. 'It is no sacrifice, James. I told Philip that Julian and I would deal well together and I really do mean it. And what do you think about Mama and Bertram? At least Julian's kind offer for me has had the effect of bringing them together. You must feel pleased.'

James nodded. 'I must confess to feeling that they were made for each other. Bertram was never right for you, Sarah. But it does not stop me from wishing that it could have been Philip.'

She looked at him mischievously. 'I had the idea that Marianne might do for Philip.'

'No, no,' he protested. 'I suggested it to him and it had never entered his mind – he thought she was still in the schoolroom! I am sure it is you he loves even if he has only just realized it. It has taken a rival to open his eyes. I think we ought to persuade him that Marianne should be the one, you will have to see what you can do, Sarah.' He did not notice her woebegone expression and went on enthusiastically: 'Philip has asked me to go to Luttons Park and help with the estate until we go to Brighton. You do not mind, Sarah?'

'It is a splendid idea,' she said more cheerfully. 'It will keep you out of mischief and from finding any more actresses.'

He gave a boyish grin. 'I don't think you will ever let me forget Crystal, will you? But I deserve it for being such a greenhorn.' He started walking back towards the house. 'I must go and get my things together. I am going to ask Reuben to take my bags to the dower house and I will ride over on Turk.'

Sarah was sorry that Julian was going to be away, but so great was her relief that she was free of having to make the decision about Bertram, that she enjoyed quiet walks up to see how Anita and Marianne were faring and rode out quite happily on her own.

Bertram was at Little Cleeve every day; he and Lady Hadlow had long talks about Marianne's come-out and the plans for their own wedding. This would be a quiet affair in September after their annual visit to Brighton. Every evening, Sarah would listen at length to what her mama had to say about 'dear Bertram'. But she was glad to listen – pleased for her mama, pleased for Bertram and also with a quiet feeling of pleasure for herself.

That was until she met Philip one afternoon when she was out riding; she was about to turn back towards Little Cleeve and he was on his way home to Luttons. It was the first time she had seen him since James had gone over to join him.

Philip wore rather a brooding look, but Sarah chose not to notice it and greeted him cheerfully.

'Hallo, Philip. I have been wanting to say thank you for taking James. It will do him good to be occupied.'

They did not dismount but faced each other across their horses' backs. 'I thought it would take his mind off his adventures with the actress,' he replied with some of the old banter back in his voice.

'Julian has taken her back to London,' Sarah told him.

'And stayed a few days with her, no doubt,' he said in quite a changed tone, and Sarah was horrified at his words.

'Philip, that is a wicked thing to say. Especially when you know I am engaged to marry Julian and I am feeling particularly grateful to him for taking Crystal off our hands. I might ask you what you would have done in the circumstances if you had been there when James and Crystal suddenly burst in on us.'

'I do not suppose for a moment that I would have welcomed Crystal de Florette into my home, but I certainly would have done my best to dissuade James from his association with her,' he replied in a stiff manner.

'Actions speak louder than words, Philip,' Sarah shot at him.

'Are you seeking a quarrel with me, Sarah?'

'No, I am not. I just wish you would be more charitable in your opinion of Julian.'

'If I am not charitable, it is because I have yet to see him do something other than to boost his own high opinion of himself. Half the time, he plays a part, I am sure of it; pretending chivalry and kindness when he schemes only to give you the idea that he is the perfect American gentleman.'

Sarah could not believe that this was her Philip. 'You hate him, Philip.'

But he shook his head vigorously. 'No, it is not hatred. I just despise his manipulation of your affairs. I do not suppose that you have seen the last of his ploys, Sarah.'

'I refuse to listen to you. You are seeing evil where there is only good and it is not the Philip I used to know.'

He leaned across and took her hand. 'Do not heed me, Sarah, it is the old green-eyed monster, jealousy, just as Iago said – do you know your *Othello*? – I have not changed at heart, but I am sore at having lost you to someone like Julian Cleeve. I will get over it sooner or late. I am the same Philip and you know that you can count on me. I am sorry for what I said if it hurts you, Sarah, for that is the last thing I would wish to do. Forgive?'

Sarah nodded, her eyes filling with tears; she could not bear to lose Philip's friendship yet she had to defend Julian. 'I did not hear any of it, Philip. You go on back to the dower house and tear our cousin's reputation to shreds with James. But I think you will find that James will take my part.'

'We will see. Goodbye, Sarah.'

'Goodbye, Philip.'

Sarah's little war of words with Philip was quickly forgotten with the events of the following morning. Bertram had not yet arrived and Sarah was sitting quietly in the drawing-room with Lady Hadlow. Sarah was trying to concentrate on Miss Austen's latest book, *Mansfield Park*, which had been recently published; but she found that she saw Philip's face rather than Edmund's and Julian's instead of the despicable Henry.

With these diversions in her mind, and the constant interruptions from Lady Hadlow who was wondering what had become of Bertram, Sarah put her book to one side and sat thinking.

The quiet was suddenly and rudely disturbed by the arrival of a sobbing Marianne. She burst into the room and flung herself at Sarah who had never seen her sister so upset.

'Whatever is it, Marianne? Try and calm yourself. . . .' And then she turned as she heard a cry come from the *chaise-longue*. 'Mama, lie back and compose yourself; please do not add to the trouble while I speak to Marianne.'

Marianne had obviously run all the way from Cleeve Grange because it was minutes before she found the breath to speak.

'Sarah, you must come and help – it is Anita – oh, poor Anita, oh what shall we do?' cried Marianne and buried her head in Sarah's lap.

Sarah spoke sternly. 'Has there been an accident? Is Anita hurt?' Then she gave Marianne a shake. 'Marianne Winterson, you will stop crying, you will sit up and then you will tell us the whole. How can we help if we do not know what is wrong? Is Anita hurt?

Shall I go to the Grange? Please begin at the beginning for nothing makes sense.'

Marianne sat up but she was very distressed. 'Anita has been kidnapped.'

Sarah lost her temper. 'Do not talk such nonsense, if you please, Marianne. Sit there and do not move and I will get you a restorative.' Sarah left the room to the sound of sobs from both her mother and her sister and then returned in seconds with the hartshorn. 'Now start at the very beginning; try and tell us exactly what has happened. We cannot help you if we do not know what the problem is. Do you understand, Marianne?'

The young girl nodded and dried her eyes; she knew her sister in this mood.

'It was not long ago: Anita and I were in the drawing-room – oh, Cousin Julian has not returned from London yet. We heard a carriage and thought it was him and we rushed to the window . . . well, it was the most broken-down old carriage I have ever seen and a man dressed quite in style sitting up in front, not in the least like a coachman. Then we heard the drawing-room door open and Jenny the maid . . . oh, you won't believe it, Sarah; it was Crystal she showed in. . . .'

Lady Hadlow gave a shriek and Sarah stared. 'Crystal de Florette? But what had she come for?'

'Wait, Sarah, wait, and I will try and tell you properly and in the right order. She still had that awful hairstyle and was wearing a bright blue pelisse—'

'But what did she want?'

'She asked for Cousin Julian and when she found that he was not there, she said, never mind, she had put a note for him on the small table in the entrance hall. Then she came out with it straight away. Had we seen her pearls – you remember, that long loop of large pearls she was wearing when she first arrived with James. She said she had lost them and thought she must have left them in her bedroom here and would I kindly go and look for them – they would be in one of the drawers for safety – while she had a chat with Anita. Oh, Sarah.' Marianne put her hands to her face. 'I will try not to cry.'

'Take your time, Marianne.' Sarah could make no sense of the story as yet.

'I was a long time looking, you know how many chests of drawers there are in the guest room. But I could not find the pearls and ran down the stairs again . . . that is when it happened. . . .'

'Go on.'

'There was no one in the drawing-room and I could not understand it . . . then I heard wheels on the gravel outside the front door and I ran to the window and there was the old carriage going down the drive as fast as it could go and looking as though a wheel was going to come off at any minute.'

Marianne faltered. '. . . I did not know what to do, Sarah. I started to run after them which was a silly thing to do – as though I could catch up with a carriage – I thought how silly I was, I had not even looked for Anita. So I ran back to the house, but she was nowhere to be seen and Mrs Stockdale and Mrs Lingfield knew nothing about it and had not seen Anita. The only thing I could think of was to come to you so I came as fast as I could . . . oh, Sarah.' And once again, Marianne threw herself at her sister who was thinking fast.

'Marianne, do not cry again. Answer my questions. When you arrived just now, you said that Anita had been kidnapped, why did you say that?'

'Well, she has. Crystal has taken her.'

'But how do you know that: they might have just gone for a drive.'

'No, no, no!' Marianne shouted, and she held out her hand. In it was a crumpled piece of paper. 'I read Crystal's note to Cousin Julian, I know I should not have done so, but I was full of panic. I had forgotten it – oh, it is all screwed up, you read it, Sarah.'

Sarah flattened the small piece of paper and glanced over the ill-formed letters. She read the words with a dawning horror.

To get Anita back please leave 500 guineas at the London house and I will bring her home the next day. She will come to no harm.

Crystal

She had not spoken aloud and her mother was crying again and almost shouting at her. 'What does it say, Sarah? Is the child safe?'

Sarah went up to the *chaise-longue*, thinking furiously as she did so. 'It is a ransom note, Mama. Crystal demands money from Cousin Julian and then she will return Anita safely . . . oh, Mama, do not swoon, please try, please try. I could wish that Bertram was here.' Then she turned to Marianne, her mind made up. 'Marianne, listen carefully. You were right to come to me. I will ride to Luttons Park and ask Bertram to come and sit with Mama: you are to stay here until he arrives. Then you are to walk back to Cleeve Grange, tell Mrs Stockdale what has happened and then stay there until Cousin Julian returns.'

'But what about Anita?' Marianne asked tremulously.

'I will go and find Philip. If we can go in his curricle, we should easily catch up with a carriage even though they have had such a good start. Try not to worry and put your trust in Philip to do his best.'

'Oh, I will, Sarah, I will do anything to help get Anita back.'

'Go round to the stables then and ask Reuben to saddle Cilla for me. I will slip into my riding-habit – Mama, you will stay calm until Bertram comes, won't you?'

Lady Hadlow nodded feebly. 'I will try, Sarah, I will try for Anita's sake,' she moaned softly, and the tears fell again.

Sarah was changed and up on Cilla in five minutes, then good fortune came her way. Another five minutes out from Little Cleeve, she saw two riders in the distance and her heart leapt when she saw that it was Philip riding with Bertram. Philip broke into a gallop and was with her in seconds.

'What is it, Sarah, is something wrong? I was coming to apologize for my words of yesterday . . . but you are distracted, tell me quickly.'

Sarah spoke as briefly as she could and then, as Bertram approached, asked him to go as quickly as possible to her mama who would tell him the whole. Then she turned to Philip. 'What shall we do, Philip?'

He had no hesitation. 'Ride back to Little Cleeve, Sarah. I will return to Luttons for my curricle; I will be as quick as I can so be ready for me. I think we can catch the carriage from the sound of it, and I shall need you there if Anita is with them. Will you do that, Sarah?'

'Thank you, Philip, thank you. I will do just as you say.'

It did not seem very long before Sarah was up beside Philip in his fast curricle and they were bowling along the lanes to Bidborough.

But the carriage was nowhere to be seen between the Grange and Bidborough; Philip had hoped they might have caught up with its slow progress along the narrow country lanes.

In Bidborough itself, a small village, they had no success with their enquiries until they reached the tavern. There was a farm cart outside and Philip ran into the low building full of hope. It was the farmer who answered his questions.

'Yes, sir, it went by not ten minutes since just as I were coming in. Having trouble, the coachman were, with a wheel nearly off; reckon he won't have got far, but he went in the direction of the London road. You'll catch him easy afore you reach Tonbridge.'

Philip was heartened by this news and they set off at great speed; but all they passed before they reached the turnpike road was a pedlar, his heavy pack nearly weighing him down.

Philip hardly came to a standstill to ask his queston of the laden man, but was off in a shot when they heard the reply.

'Won't reach Tonbridge, that'un, wheel nearly off.'

Sarah smiled for the first time. 'We might catch them yet,' she said.

They were only half a mile along the Tonbridge road when they saw the carriage and Sarah gave a little scream. For it was lying at a tilt in the ditch, the wheel had come off and the horse was missing.

'Philip,' said Sarah. 'They might have tied Anita up inside and made their escape on the horse. . . .'

But Philip had jumped down from the curricle and was climbing over the fallen carriage.

'Anita,' he called as loudly as he could, but there was no answering cry. Sarah joined him and Philip forced open the door. They were loooking into a shabby, threadbare carriage which was quite empty.

Silently they climbed back on to the curricle. 'Now what can we do?' asked Sarah, in a small and disappointed voice.

Philip was thinking fast and speaking urgently. 'The horse is missing so they must have ridden off on it, but they would never get three of them on a beast like that.'

'And they would need a wheelwright,' Sarah said.

'Yes, I can only make sense of it if the coachman has ridden for a wheelwright, and left Crystal to take care of Anita somewhere. They are probably in a tavern or a farmhouse if there is one along this road. We must set off, Sarah, and call at every dwelling that we pass.'

She nodded in agreement, but was losing heart and she was very quiet as she sat with Philip on the curricle once again.

There were few buildings as they were going through farmland and the most they could hope for was an isolated farmhouse.

When they saw two small cottages, low and poor looking, Sarah began to hope. In each one, Philip found a woman with small children gathered round her skirts, but they both disclaimed seeing anyone on a horse. The first woman was taciturn, the second more helpful and suggested they might try at Goddards farm down the road.

Philip drove the curricle more quickly and round the next bend, a farmhouse came into view. It was not large but looked respectable – set off the road with a tidy vegetable garden in front of it.

Philip jumped down and knocked at the solid oak door. A neat servant answered.

'Is your mistress in?' he asked

'Mrs Goddard? Oh yes, sir, such a to-do as we've had.'

Eight

PHILIP TURNED TO Sarah and she jumped down to join him. They were shown into a small but neat parlour where they were joined only seconds later by a flustered little woman who said she was Mrs Goddard.

Philip made a bow. 'Philip Hesslewood, brother to Sir Bertram Hesslewood of Luttons Park; this is the Hon Miss Sarah Winterson of Cleeve.'

Mrs Goddard's expression was a little less worried. 'Your brother Sir Bertram, sir? He comes this way hunting very often. But how can I help you? As if I've not had enough trouble this morning already.'

Sarah felt excited as though they were at last on the right scent, but she let Philip do the talking.

'I am sorry to hear it, Mrs Goddard. I have come to enquire if you have seen anyone on horseback pass this morning? Not very long ago, in fact.'

'They was here,' said Mrs Goddard and then could not stop talking. 'Right pretty woman, dressed something grand; it was she as did all the talking. He were a right silent one, her husband were and the little girl was very quiet, looked frightened, I thought. In a fix they was, too, for their carriage had lost a wheel and gone in a ditch a little way back, so she said. And could I help them out?

They was taking the nipper, respectable young girl she looked, back to London to her stepmother's. Seems she had run away from home and had gone to Tunbridge Wells where she had relations; on the stagecoach, too, the naughty girl. So Mr and Mrs Smith had offered to fetch her home and they'd found her all right. But she didn't like it at her aunt's so she agreed to go back with them. Well, what was I to do, I said? Would I let her stay here while they went on the horse to find a wheelwright for the carriage? Of course I would, I said, poor little pet even if she had been naughty to run away; she can stay in the spare bedroom, it's not cold weather . . .'

Sarah was impatient to get to Anita for she had no doubt that it was Anita herself up in the spare bedroom, but she could not stop Mrs Goddard.

'. . . well, they was all thanks and we took the little one upstairs and she didn't make no fuss, just sat on the bed as quiet as a mouse. "We won't be long, Anita", said Mrs Smith, "but we'll have to lock you in, don't want you running off again. You'll be all right along of Mrs Goddard till we get the carriage mended". And there she is, up in the best bedroom with the door locked so I can't even take her a bite because they took the key and there's no knowing how long they'll be . . . so that's the story and it's enough trouble for one morning, I reckon.'

Sarah and Philip looked at each other, Sarah feeling very confident. Anita was here and quite safe, even if she was locked in. It would be a long time before Crystal returned, if she came back at all and they would have Anita safely home by that time. But first they had to convince the good farmer's wife.

Sarah spoke for the first time. 'Mrs Goddard, you have believed everything that Mrs Smith told you, but I must now convince you that it as all a pack of lies and that the young lady is Miss Anita Cleeve. She is my cousin. She has been kidnapped by the Smiths – that is not their name – and we set off as quickly as we could to try and catch up with the carriage. But, of course, we found it in the ditch.' She turned to Philip and he nodded. 'Please take us to Miss Cleeve. She will recognize us straight away and will convince you of the true story.'

'Oh, I believe you, miss.' Mrs Goddard looked as though she was about to burst into tears. 'I thought as something havey-cavey was going on and Mrs Smith dressed rather vulgar. But, miss, the door is locked. It's the best bedroom in the house and the only one with a lock and key . . . oh dear me, what shall we do?'

Philip was already out of the room and climbing the stairs, Sarah following on his heels. 'I will break the door down, Mrs Goddard, and Anita's father will provide you with a new one, I promise you. Show me the room, please.'

Upstairs, Mrs Goddard pointed to a door, which indeed had a lock, but it did not look as if it had been made of very solid wood.

'Anita,' cried Sarah. 'Anita, are you there? It is Sarah and I have Philip with me.'

They heard a shout from inside the room and a banging on the door. 'Sarah, oh Sarah, I knew you would come. I guessed that Marianne would fetch you.'

'Stand right away from the door, Anita, I am going to knock it in,' shouted Philip.

The door gave at the first push of his strong shoulder and, seconds later, Anita was in Sarah's arms.

'I didn't cry, Sarah, not once. But however did you find me? That wicked Crystal.'

Mrs Goddard was beaming at them. 'Well I never, you really is cousins. Now come down in the parlour and I will fetch some wine. It will restore you, Miss Anita, and to think of the tale that Mrs Smith told as bold as brass. And I believed every word.'

Sarah and Philip both laughed and it was as much a laugh of relief as at the expression on Mrs Goddard's face. 'She is an actress, Mrs Goddard,' said Anita. 'Her name is Miss Florette.'

'And I reckon that's not her real name neither,' said Mrs Goddard.

'No, it is Martha Suggit,' said Sarah, and over their wine, they laughed afresh.

The wine brought colour to Anita's cheeks and the sparkle back into her eyes. 'What will we do now?' she asked them.

'We will get you back to Cleeve Grange as fast as we can for we have left Marianne in a great worry.'

In no time, they were back through Bidborough and going down the drive of Cleeve Grange. There appeared to be a welcome party at the front door. Marianne was there, together with Mrs Stockdale, Mrs Lingfield and John Capel.

There were hugs and kisses all round and Mrs Lingfield set out a nuncheon in the breakfast-room. Anita had got over her fright and seemed to enjoy being the centre of attention. It was Marianne who asked the all-important question.

'Anita, I know I was gone quite a long time because I could not find the pearls – on reflection, I don't suppose for a minute that Crystal left them here – but however did she manage to get you into the carriage in the first place?'

Anita spoke quite cheerfully. 'I did not suspect anything. As soon as you left the room, Marianne, Crystal told me that Alfred – whom she called her town beau – was driving the carriage for her. He had not liked to come in, but would I go out with her to meet him. She had known him an age, she said. Well, I didn't especially want to meet her Alfred but neither did I want to offend her. I went out to the carriage and he was standing by the door; he made a polite bow over my hand. . . .' She stopped, and Sarah spoke quickly, 'Do not tell us if it is hard for you, Anita.'

Anita shook her head. 'No, it is not that it is hard; I am trying to work out exactly what happened. One second Alfred was making his bow, the next there was a thick kind of shawl over my head – I suppose Crystal did that, they must have had it all worked out –

and Alfred lifted me into the carriage. I was struggling and Crystal was speaking, then Alfred must have jumped into the driving seat for we were off.' She looked round her and saw that they were all listening intently.

'As soon as we got going, and a rattly old carriage it was too, Crystal took the shawl away and began to talk to me. I just sat still and listened, I wasn't frightened. It was just that I did not understand until she told me. She said that she and Alfred were going to take me to their house in London and when they received the money from Papa, they would bring me home again; she said it would only be for a day.' She looked round the table before she said her next words.

'She was a wicked person, wasn't she, Sarah? It was a kidnap, I know that now.'

'Yes, she was a wicked person, Anita, to kidnap you and demand money from your papa. She left a note, you know, telling Cousin Julian how to get you back. Crystal knew that he would pay any amount to have you safely home.'

'But she did not look wicked,' Anita mused. 'I thought wicked people would look mean and ugly. But she was quite droll in those vulgar dresses and the plumes in her hair. It is a bit of a puzzle.'

'Crystal was a greedy woman, I think,' said Sarah. 'She was also a good actress. What happened then, Anita?'

'Crystal talked to me quite nicely. I wasn't ill-treated, some things she said quite made me laugh. But the carriage started a wobble and Alfred shouted something about the wheel. Crystal became quiet and the wobbling got worse and worse until we were tipped right over and came to a halt. We weren't hurt at all. Alfred helped me out and all I could do was stand there and look at the carriage in the ditch and wonder what they would do next. It was no good me running away for I had not the least idea where we were and it was all fields and trees and no houses in sight.'

'Weren't you frightened then?' Marianne asked.

Anita shook her head. 'No, it seemed like a prank to me. Being kidnapped and then the carriage breaking down not far from home. I was sure that someone would catch up with us. Alfred unhitched the horse and he said he would ride it and I was to walk with Crystal, he thought he could see a farmhouse in the distance.' She gave a chuckle.

'The next part was like a charade until they locked me in. Mrs Goddard, the woman at the farm, was very nice and she believed every word that Crystal told her. How I'd run away from home and they were taking me back to London and would Mrs Goddard keep me there while they went on the horse to try and find a wheelwright. But I could see that was a Canterbury tale for I guessed they would make off and not come back. I was put in the best bedroom which was quite comfortable so I just sat on the bed and waited. I felt sure that someone would come and it did not seem long.' She turned to Sarah. 'Papa will be angry, won't he, Sarah?'

Sarah tried to sound reassuring. 'I think he will be very relieved that you have come to no harm, Anita. When do you expect him back?'

'I thought it would be some time today,' replied Anita. 'I wish he was here.'

Sarah turned to Philip. 'I will wait for a while with the girls, Philip. Could you go and tell Mama of a happy outcome? I will walk round to the stables with you.'

At the stables, the two of them stood by the curricle and Sarah put her hand on Philip's arm. 'Thank you for all you have done, Philip, please know that I appreciate it.'

He kissed her lightly on the cheek and she reached up and kissed him back. 'We need not always be at odds, Sarah, I am glad it has turned out well.'

And it was upon this scene, that the Cleeve Grange carriage swept round the corner of the house and Julian stepped down from it, looked about him and frowned then walked up quickly to Philip and Sarah.

'Are you playing me false, by any chance, Sarah?' he asked and for Julian, it was said somewhat impatiently.

'I must tell you, Cleeve . . .' began Philip, but Sarah, fearing a disagreement between the two men, interrupted hastily.

'Julian, I am glad to see you at home for we have had a lot of trouble in your absence.'

'Trouble?' he said shortly. 'What do you mean?'

'I will not tell you anything for Anita will want to tell you herself.'

'Anita?' Is she all right?' he asked harshly.

'Yes, she is quite all right now but she has had rather an ordeal at the hands of Miss Crystal de Florette.'

Julian frowned and looked embarrassed. 'Crystal? What has she to do with the matter? I took her back to London.'

'I want you to hear it from Anita herself so have patience. Philip has kindly assisted us and I am just quietly thanking him and seeing him on his way. I will come back into the house with you now. Goodbye, Philip, and thank you again.'

'Goodbye, my Sarah,' said Philip, then flicked his whip and drove off.

'And what was that supposed to mean? "My Sarah" indeed,' said Julian irritably.

Sarah laughed and she thought it must be the first laugh of the day. 'I have been "my Sarah" to Philip since I learned to talk, you do not need to read anything into it.'

'So I should hope. What is all this about Anita and Crystal?'

'Come along in and let her tell you herself; she was wishing that you were here.'

At the front of Cleeve Grange, Anita, having been told that the carriage had arrived, was on the steps and flew into Julian's arms.

Neither of them said a word, but Sarah had the disturbing

impression that they clung to each other like lovers reunited. Then she shook her head and called herself foolish; Anita is all that Julian has in the world, she thought.

In the drawing-room, refreshment was brought and Julian listened with a stony expression while Anita told her tale. She had recovered from the shock of her experience and made it all sound like a big adventure. But Julian was grim-faced and held on to her hand tightly.

At the end of her narration, Anita looked round at her audience and at Julian in particular. 'And that is all. It wasn't a very exciting kidnap, was it? Not like in the novels of Mrs Radcliffe you have let me read since I have been here, Marianne.' She turned to Julian. 'What happens now, Papa?'

Julian was thoughtful. 'First of all, I think we have seen the last of Miss Crystal de Florette. She will not show her face or demand money for fear of being taken into custody for attempted kidnap. Alfred might try and retrieve his carriage, though it sounds as though it is not worth mending. And I must go along and see the excellent Mrs Goddard and arrange to have her best bedroom door replaced. Then we must forget all about the incident and concentrate on the come-out ball.'

He got up and walked round to where Sarah was sitting. 'I will walk back to Little Cleeve with you, Sarah. I have to thank you for all that you have done.'

'And Philip,' she added.

'Maybe, maybe not,' he replied.

Julian walked slowly with Sarah down the drive to Little Cleeve. As she walked, Sarah felt in harmony with her cousin and pleased to be engaged to him.

'Julian, you lost no time in getting Crystal back to London,' she said to him and then she thought of Philip's words and immediately regretted the remembrance. Philip had been in an ill humour at the time of his remark, but his help in rescuing Anita seemed to have restored them to their old friendship. But it made her wonder how Crystal had behaved with Julian and whether she had tried to extract more money from him. 'However did you manage?'

'No trouble at all,' he replied. 'I am sure I do not know when I have been so entertained – and it is not every day that a gentleman has the opportunity of escorting a woman of the town to London.'

'Oh, dear, was she so dreadful?'

'Appallingly awful; she seems to be motivated by money,' he said.

'Was it a big sum, Cousin?' Sarah asked rather apprehensively.

'A shocking amount. She is a very expensive lady, except of course that I cannot call her a lady. It was worth every penny to travel up to London in her company. It gave me an insight into a part of English society, I knew only existed from the more scurrilous prints!'

'James will pay it somehow, I will make sure of that.'

'You will do no such thing, Sarah. I want to ask him to persuade Anita to ride again. And Anita has come to no harm which is the most important thing, I think she quite enjoyed being the centre of attention, don't you?'

Sarah gave a little laugh. 'I think she did. She is going to enjoy the girls' come-out ball.'

'Before this affair with Crystal, they were talking of nothing else. I must ask you, Sarah, do you dance the waltz? I look forward to having you in my arms and whirling you around the ballroom.'

Sarah could see the good humour in his face and guessed that her next remark would vex him. 'I *do* dance the waltz, but I am not sure that I will be at the come-out ball.'

They were almost at Little Cleeve. Julian stopped short, his hand shooting out to grasp her arm as in a vice.

'Are you saying it just to make me angry? Would you care to

explain yourself in case I did not hear you aright the first time?'

'I am afraid I will not be at the come-out ball,' she persisted.

'So I did hear you correctly. Would you please tell me what you mean by such a preposterous statement? You know that the ball will be for Marianne as well as for Anita and Jane; not only that, I will be able to present you as my betrothed. It will serve as an engagement celebration.'

Sarah could feel herself growing angry because she knew that she would never make her cousin understand.

'I have no suitable gown for a ball,' she said stubbornly.

'But it is three weeks away yet; you have time to purchase one,' he objected.

Sarah's heart sank. She knew very well what would happen if she told him that any money she had available would have to be saved for a gown for her mama's wedding to Bertram which they planned for September.

She tried hard. 'It will be hard for you to understand for you do not know what it is to be purse-pinched. I do have a little money, but it must be spent on my gown for Mama's wedding; I cannot buy a ballgown, as well. Mama and I have talked it over and we have decided that she will be the family representative at Marianne's come-out. She has a gown which has put in many appearances, but with a few new ribbons, it will serve . . . no, no, Julian, do not argue. My mind is made up and I do not wish us to quarrel.'

Julian had now possessed himself of her hands. He was almost speechless . . . but not quite.

'Sarah, my sweet love, you know I will purchase a gown for you . . .' he began, but before he had finished his sentence, he knew he had said the wrong thing.

Sarah tore her hands from his grasp and faced him angrily. 'Julian Cleeve, you may be my cousin and my betrothed, but I will not suffer the indignity of you providing a gown for me. Bertram would never have made the offer if he had been in your place. I will have you know that in this country it is only a certain class of woman who would allow a gentleman to provide her with a gown. I am Sarah Winterson; and I am not Miss Crystal de Florette. You bought her off successfully and obviously enjoyed her company in London; perhaps you are thinking you can do the same with me. You are . . . oh, words cannot describe it. . . .' And she turned away from him in anger and started to run towards Little Cleeve.

'Sarah, wait . . . please wait. No, stay still and listen to me. Please, please, Sarah, stop struggling. I am not going to hurt you, I only ask you to listen to me.'

'You are a beast,' she shouted at him for she could not match his strength and she was doing her best not to show the tears of her humiliation and anger.

'My little love. . . .'

'I am not your little love; you do not love me any more than I love you.'

'I suppose it is the estimable Philip you think you love,' he said with a certain bitterness.

'I will not listen to such remarks; you are no better than Philip. Two grown gentlemen fighting over me as if I was a child's toy.' Sarah looked at him and saw a disagreeable expression come into his eyes.

'I won you though, Sarah.' There was an edge to his voice.

'I daresay you did and do not think I am going to cry off. The arrangement suited me at the time and I have had no cause to reconsider my decision. Philip's heart is lost in the past and I do not think you have any heart at all; you like arranging things to suit yourself.'

'Little shrew.'

'You have called me that before. I was always of a shrewish temper and you will learn to get used to it. We maybe both have our faults, but I think we suit each other.' Sarah could not remember when she had behaved so badly but there was something in her cousin which seemed to provoke her uncertain temper.

'I suppose you are right, Sarah, but what about this business of the ball? You know that it would be very remiss of you not to attend.'

Sarah knew she would have to give in, it would hurt too many people if she did not attend. 'Very well,' she surrendered. 'There are some nice silks in the sewing-room at the Grange if you will let me choose something, and Marianne will help me make a gown.'

'Thank you, Sarah,' he said quietly, and looked at her searchingly.

'You really mean it, do you not? You are a strange mixture of a man, but I daresay I will enjoy dancing the waltz with you. You need come no further, Julian. Thank you for walking back with me.'

'It is you I have to thank, Sarah, you and Philip Hesslewood, damn him. He is too familiar with you for comfort. But I trust you, Sarah. Let me give you a kiss.' He bent down and quickly touched her lips, no more, and Sarah hurried into the house to see if her mama had survived the worry and the excitement.

By the time the incident of Miss Crystal de Florette and the kidnap was only an amusing memory and James had settled into Luttons Park with Philip, there remained only a few days until the girls' come-out ball.

Marianne and Anita moved into Tunbridge Wells to be with Jane and at the same time, Jane's older brother, Oliver arrived on the scene. Oliver was a full seven years older than Jane and was the only one of her brothers not yet married. He had read law at Oxford, hoped to become a barrister, and was comfortably settled as a lawyer in London; he had recently become betrothed to Miss

Hester Brewer, the daughter of one of the senior partners in his chambers.

Oliver, at five-and-twenty, was a serious young man and Jane considered him to have become yet more serious since his betrothal to Hester. Oliver used to be fun, Jane was wont to say, until he met Hester who was a tall, rather striking girl, older than him by three years. Now almost thirty years of age, it was her height and her small inexpressive eyes that were remembered by anyone meeting her. She had endured several unsuccessful seasons and the arrival of the handsome Oliver Humphries in London, and his introduction into the Brewers' big London house by her father, provoked her into making a play for his affections.

As she was wealthy from a legacy left to her by a godmother and would provide him with a good opportunity for furthering his career, Oliver fell prey to her flattering attentions. He did not love her but considered – sometimes rather ruefully – that marriages of convenience were often successful ones.

That was before he came home into Kent for his sister's come-out ball.

Two days before the ball, all the families and friends of Jane, Marianne and Anita met for dinner at the Humphries' house in Tunbridge Wells before going on to see the play at the theatre in the Pantiles. This imposing building had been built in 1802 by Mrs Sarah Baker, a flamboyant character who took her touring company around Kent and called her theatre the Temple of the Muses.

It was a happy party who gathered in the drawing-room before dinner and it was on this scene that Oliver arrived from London bringing Hester Brewer with him. Sarah was not surprised that Oliver was a good-looking young man, but the alliance with Hester seemed unfortunate, she thought.

Hester was dressed in a sober, grey, high-necked gown with no jewellery to lighten it; her dark hair was swept up with no escaping ringlets and contrived to give her a rather forbidding look.

Indeed, she was unbearably formal in her manner when the introductions were made. 'I am very pleased that Jane has such good young friends,' she said to Sarah, after she had spoken to Anita and Marianne. 'She is inclined to be hoydenish being the youngest of the family and growing up with older brothers. But I am sure your sister has been very properly brought up, Miss Winterson. I see that she is talking to Oliver now; he looks very tall beside her, does he not?'

Sarah had been watching Marianne and Oliver out of the corner of her eye while Hester had been making her rather starchy remarks and saw that they were laughing easily together, as though they were old friends. They only met five minutes ago, Sarah was thinking, I hope that Marianne does not do something foolish like falling in love with him. Miss Brewer is very formidable and I do not think she would take kindly to a flirtation between her betrothed and his sister's young friend.

Hester moved away to join Oliver and her place was taken at Sarah's side by Julian. Sarah thought that he had one of his slightly wicked smiles about him and wondered what outrageous remark he would come out with.

'Sarah, my dear, so many of us and I have not had a chance to speak to you. I see you were talking to the new arrival from London. What do you think? Ill-suited, are they not? Oliver seems to be a lively young man who has been subdued by the company he keeps. As for Hester – I can only describe her as being very old-maidish in spite of being betrothed to Oliver.'

Sarah looked at him suspiciously. 'You are not match-making again, are you, Julian?'

He leaned close to her and whispered in her ear. 'I had the thought that perhaps Bertram and Hester would make a pair! Don't you agree? Look, they are talking together now.'

Sarah was incensed. 'You have a short memory, Cousin. Have you forgotten that my mama is betrothed to Bertram?'

He gave a mock sigh. 'I always forget and yet it was of my making, was it not?'

'You like your own way in things, I believe,' returned Sarah.

'Oh dear, you are in a serious mood, just when I fancied a little flirtation,' he replied, and in such a tone that she could not stop herself from laughing.

'If you feel flirtatious, go and try your wiles on Hester. It would brighten her up; she seems rather a sour-puss to me.'

'Vixen,' he said, and lifted her hand to his lips. 'But I will do as you say. Just watch me.'

And Sarah saw him join Hester and Bertram who were standing together.

'I hope I may call you Hester,' said Julian blandly. 'I must say that it is very nice that you and Oliver can be with us for the ball. I know that Jane is most fond of her brother. Tell me, do you stand up for the waltz?'

Hester gave a slight frown. 'I do not, Mr Cleeve,' she replied, rather pointedly not using his first name. 'My mama thinks it is most improper and I agree with her. I have no doubt you dance the waltz?'

'Oh yes; I did not think it would be frowned upon in Tunbridge Wells.'

Bertram had listened with some pleasure to Hester's comments and suddenly intervened. 'Miss Brewer, I wholeheartedly agree with you. I do not stand up for the waltz and neither does Lady Hadlow. What about Mr Humphries? What is his opinion?'

Sarah had been joined by Philip but she saw Hester's lips tighten. 'He will do as I wish, of course,' Miss Brewer said.

Philip had heard the end of the conversation, too, and his eyes met Sarah's and there was silent laughter between them.

Sarah was pleased to speak to Philip for she had seen him across the room and her heart had stirred at how handsome he looked. She was used to seeing him dressed for the life he led out of doors and was jolted into admiration at his appearance in his evening clothes. He wore fashionable tight-fitting trousers of ivory-white velvet strapped under the instep. The waistcoat was to match. His evening dress-coat was of superbly fitting lavender cloth and Sarah thought that Julian could not match him for elegance.

'I feel put out,' he said to her and she knew from his tone that he was roasting her; they had managed not to quarrel during the time since Anita's kidnap and she was pleased to be on good terms with him once again.

'Not jealousy again, Philip,' she joked.

'I am *always* jealous when I see you with Cleeve, but I still live in hope.'

'Hope of what?'

'Hope that he will try one scheme too many and that your fine romance will collapse.' Philip spoke very quietly and Sarah was not quite sure if he was quizzing her or not.

But she had the impression that he was serious and she almost hissed her reply. 'You are outrageous and I will not listen to you. And you have not told me why you feel put out.'

'My sweet Sarah, have you not seen Marianne with Oliver Humphries? And you promised her to me on this occasion.'

She gave a little frown. 'I have seen them together and they look as though they are made for each other, I must admit. But I will have to do something, for Marianne should not make up to Oliver when he is engaged to Hester.'

Philip laughed. 'I think the partners are becoming a little confused; Hester seems quite taken with Bertram, or the other way round.'

'Oh dear,' sighed Sarah. 'But it is a social gathering and we are obliged to circulate amongst our friends. Perhaps you could rescue Marianne, Philip.'

'I will try,' he promised.

Nine

WHILE THIS CONVERSATION was going on, Anita was apart with James, and Oliver was sitting with his sister and Marianne; they were all talking and laughing together.

Oliver was dressed very modestly in grey pantaloons under a coat of blue superfine and his waistcoat was also grey; his neck-cloth was the most elegant thing about him, an intricate fall of white linen lightly starched. With Hester, he had looked stiff and serious, but sitting at ease with Jane and Marianne, his expression had lightened and his mouth curved in a smile.

Marianne was used to seeing James dressed to the nines, but Oliver Humphries had the extra years which gave a polish lacking in James. After a few moments of conversation, she realized that he was addressing his remarks to her and she responded without coyness.

'You puzzle me, Marianne,' he was saying. 'I lived all that time here in Tunbridge Wells before I went up to Oxford, how could I have missed meeting you if you were living at Cleeve Grange?'

Marianne looked very pretty that evening. Her muslin dress was simple, but it was a pale-blue with deeper blue ribbons at the waist and the flounce of the hem. Oliver, used to the staid propriety of Hester, was fascinated and his fascination made him forget that his betrothed was only an arm's length away.

'But, Oliver,' replied Marianne, 'you must not forget that Jane and I are almost the same age, so that the time you are remembering – which must be over six years ago – I would still have been in the schoolroom. After that, my father died and left us sadly dipped, so I was never able to go to any routs or parties in Tunbridge Wells. This is my first season.'

'I do remember stories of your father gambling rather heavily,' he said thoughtfully, but then he smiled at her. 'But if I had known you were there, I would have come and taken you out of the schoolroom and we could have gone galloping over the fields together!'

'You are roasting me,' she replied prettily. 'You would have gone off to Oxford without giving me another thought. And now you have Hester.'

Her remark seemed to shake him. 'Good God, I had forgot Hester for a moment, your blue eyes have me bewitched. I had better see what she is about; she is probably talking propriety to someone. But tell me one thing, Marianne: do you dance the waltz? Hester does not approve, but I love to waltz, so please save it for me at the ball.'

'I think we had better wait and see what Hester says,' said Marianne, knowing by now that nothing would give her greater delight than to dance the waltz with Oliver Humphries.

'You are very proper,' he smiled, and moved across the room, Marianne's eyes following him.

'I think you have made a hit with my brother,' said Jane. 'I have not seen him so playful for a long time. Not since he met Hester, in fact. I cannot like her, Marianne. I will tell you in confidence because you are my friend. I know she is very dignified and is a suitable match for Oliver, but one has to be on one's best behaviour when she visits. She describes me as hoydenish!'

Marianne laughed. 'They will be living in London, Jane, and it is possible you will receive an offer in your first season. You will have no need to be in a worry about them.'

'I only want to receive an offer from someone if I love him,' said Jane in her outspoken way. 'I do not want to be like Oliver and Hester, I am sure he does not love her. I could wish it was you he is going to marry.'

Marianne gave a merry laugh. 'What will you say next, Jane? Please do not repeat that to anyone else.'

'No, of course not. I think it is time to go into dinner.'

It was a very successful visit to the theatre. The finest actors always appeared at the Temple of the Muses in Tunbridge Wells. Edmund Kean had been among them until he made his début and his name at London's Drury Lane in the same play – *The Merchant of Venice* – that the Humphries party were to see that night.

They all hated Shylock and admired a very fine Portia, and in the interval between the play and the farce – which ended the evening – there was much discussion.

Sarah endured a lecture from Bertram on the character of the Jew and then turned with relief to Julian who she found was watching her with a sardonic smile as though to say 'I rescued you from all that, Sarah'.

'Sir Bertram is very knowledgeable, Sarah,' said her cousin very seriously.

But Sarah, that night, was short on patience and good manners, in rather a worry about Marianne's behaviour. 'I know you to be roasting me. Bertram can be a bore, but Mama does not seem to think so. Look at them together now, and with Hester, too, while Oliver is naughtily taken up with Jane and Marianne. I hope that Marianne is not encouraging a flirtation; she knows that Oliver is spoken for.'

The three girls had Oliver, James and Philip in attendance and they were having a most enjoyable time.

Marianne was looking shyly at Oliver and felt as though she was falling in love for the first time. And it would have to be with someone who is already spoken for, she thought sadly. But I must not encourage him, she told herself, or I will have frosty looks from Hester, and rightly so.

But Oliver was drawn to Marianne as with the irresistible force of a magnet. He was content to leave Hester with Lady Hadlow and the wealthy farmer, as he thought of Bertram, and to stand close to Marianne's chair engaging her in conversation.

'You are by far the prettiest of the three of you, Marianne,' he said softly.

She glanced up into laughing, admiring eyes and knew this to be a flirtation. Her first one.

'You like to flatter, Mr Humphries,' she answered quickly.

'Mr Humphries? I am sure you called me Oliver earlier on this evening.'

'It was rather forward of me, Oliver.' Her smile was coquettish.

'But I like you to be forward, it is refreshing. I fear I am growing old in my ways.' His tone was rueful.

'You are only four-and-twenty in my calculations, you cannot call that old precisely.'

'It is when I look at you young ladies; it makes me feel as though life has passed me by.'

Marianne felt a trifle disturbed by this remark and was not afraid of saying so. 'That is not very complimentary to Hester,' she half scolded him.

He laid his hand briefly on her shoulder in what was meant to be a careless gesture, but it came as a caress to Marianne and she felt herself give a little shiver. This is dangerous, she told herself, I must get him back to Hester.

'Oliver, poor Hester will be bored with Bertram. He is a good man but very prosaic. I think you had better go and rescue her.'

Oliver felt that he wanted to put his lips to the place on Marianne's shoulder where his fingers had been, and he hurried away to Hester's side alarmed at the strength of his feelings. I had better not go near Marianne again, he was saying to himself, she is a little temptress though she does not know it. I cannot avoid her at the ball, but after that I must return to London and forget all about her.

On their return from the theatre, Sarah and Marianne were talking together in Sarah's bedroom at the Humphries' house. Marianne had been unusually subdued and Sarah could guess why, though she hardly dared ask the question.

'What is wrong, Marianne, you are very quiet?' her sister enquired gently.

Marianne did not reply at once; she was still in her gown and sitting on Sarah's bed, making no attempt to go to her own room.

Sarah tried again. 'Is it something to do with Oliver Humphries?'

Marianne's head shot up; her expression was a perplexing mixture of pleasure and guilt. 'How did you know, Sarah? I was trying hard not to show my feelings.'

'I expect it is because I know you so well, I doubt anyone else would have noticed. You liked Oliver?'

'Oh, Sarah. . . .' There were tears in Marianne's eyes. 'He was everything I have dreamed of finding in a gentleman. Not just that he is handsome, but he was so nice to me and he made me laugh. I felt so easy with him, and I know that I should not have liked him so much because of Hester. I feel I have found someone and lost them again all in the space of one evening and . . . oh, Sarah.' And the young girl threw herself into Sarah's arms and sobbed uncontrollably.

Sarah held her young sister and let her cry. Then she spoke quietly. 'Marianne, I too saw what a pleasant young man Oliver Humphries was, but I must impress on you that you will meet many more young men like him and they will not all be engaged to someone else. I liked Oliver but he is committed to Hester and we must wish him happy.'

'I did not like Hester,' said Marianne flatly.

'She did seem to be rather a serious person, but I am sure she will make Oliver a good wife.' Then Sarah wished she had not said the words for they produced a fresh outbreak of sobbing and she knew she must be firmer with Marianne.

'Try and stop crying, Marianne, the world is not lost because of Oliver Humphries and you do not want to appear at your come-out with red eyes. I think you will be the belle of the ball in any case!'

Marianne sat up and wiped her eyes, giving Sarah a wan smile. 'You are right, Sarah, and I am being foolish. You are a good sister to me and you are fortunate in loving Julian, I am so glad he came here.'

Sarah found that Marianne's last words would not be banished as she lay awake, waiting for sleep, a few minutes later. Did she love Julian? She was certainly happy enough to be engaged to him, for she enjoyed his company and also the little sparring matches of words that they exchanged. It seemed to her to be a very light-hearted betrothal, and she somehow thought that love did not come into it.

Why these days did her thoughts turn so much to Philip? She had enjoyed the few pleasant words with him that evening, but underneath his lighter mood, she could somehow sense a touch of melancholy. Whether it was still for Clara or whether his heart was turning towards her, she could not tell; she could scarcely search out the truth from her own heart.

Not for the first time, she drifted into sleep with thoughts of both Julian and Philip and somehow was unable to separate them in her affections.

There was great excitement on the day of the ball for it was also Jane's birthday. Sir Roger had kindly asked all the Wintersons to stay and with Julian Cleeve and Anita there as well, the big house on London Road was full, noisy and happy.

Carriages took them all to the Assembly Rooms which, while not as imposing as Bath or York, glittered with chandeliers and made a perfect setting. All the ton of Tunbridge Wells were gathered for this special occasion for Sir Roger was well-known in the town. The idea of combining the come-out of three local girls had an appeal which brought fine gowns and handsomely dressed gentlemen together for the ball.

Marianne, Anita and Jane admitted to feeling nervous, but soon overcame their shyness when the introductions had been made and they found themselves receiving many flattering compliments. All three of them wore white as was the custom, but had decided between them to wear sashes and ribbons of an individual colour. Anita and Jane agreed generously that Marianne should be the one to wear blue and she had blue flowers entwined in her hair; Anita, with her dark hair, chose a pale primrose colour which became her and Jane happily settled for pink.

They all wore long white gloves and carried dainty reticules which were a present from Sir Roger.

Lady Hadlow knew the Humphries from the old, more prosperous, days and sat in a corner contentedy chatting with Lady Elizabeth with Sir Bertram and Sir Roger, delighting in criticizing – or admiring, as the case might be – the various gowns on show amongst their acquaintances. It was not Almacks, but Tunbridge Wells had its own name for elegance and style from the time in the previous century when Beau Nash had brought it to fame.

Sarah was standing with Julian waiting for the first dance, which was to be the country dance, to be announced.

'Julian,' she whispered, 'Bertram has persuaded Mama to join the set and she looks so happy. Is it not diverting?'

'Perhaps they will waltz together too,' he rejoined and she knew he was funning. 'Do not forget that you are promised to me for the first waltz.'

'No, I look forward to it.' Sarah had been watching Marianne and was pleased to see that she was behaving very properly. 'I think Philip is going to ask Marianne for the first dance, I hope he will manage to keep her away from Oliver. Do you know the young man who is dancing with Jane?'

'I don't know him, but I believe him to be the son of Lord Sudbury and a neighbour of the Humphries.'

'Just right for Jane,' said Sarah.

He looked down at her with a grin. 'Are you determined to see everyone properly paired off?' he asked.

'Well, Oliver is with Hester so that is all right, and it leaves James for Anita. Does that please you?'

'Yes, it does . . . come along, my goose, it is our turn to go down the set.'

Two waltzes were danced that evening and the partners changed for the waltz, but not before a disagreement between Oliver and his betrothed.

'Hester,' said Oliver and his voice somehow lacked enthusiasm, 'will you change your mind and dance the waltz with me?'

Hester was dressed in a stylish gown, but it was a pale green in colour and it did not become her; it was cut fashionably low in the bodice but it obviously offended her sense of what she considered modest for she wore it with a chemisette of white frilled lace. This was high to the neck and covered what would otherwise have been a daring décolletage not in the least in Hester's style.

They were all in a group waiting for the music to strike up for the waltz and Hester's chilly reply to Oliver's civil question was heard by all.

'You know my views on the waltz very well, Oliver. Perhaps you would be good enough to sit with me and your parents while those who wish it go round the floor in what I consider to be a disgraceful fashion.'

'But, Hester . . .' Oliver started to say.

'My mind is made up, Oliver, and I think it is impolite of you to argue with me when we are in company.'

The young people stared at each other quite at a loss and feeling embarrassed; Sarah wondered if she could make peace between the two of them and she looked at Julian, who simply shook his head. It was Bertram who came to the rescue.

'My dear Hester,' he said very formally. 'My views on the waltz are the same as yours. Please do come and sit out the waltz with me and Lady Hadlow. Look, here is little Marianne, let Oliver take her hand if he wishes to dance.'

Sarah drew a breath of relief and looked gratefully at Bertram. 'It is kind of you, Bertram, very kind indeed,' she said, and tried to avoid the look of joy on Marianne's face.

The waltz was announced and Sarah put her hand into Julian's. 'I thought we were going to have trouble for a moment,' she said to him.

'Be quiet,' was all his reply. 'I do not often have the chance of putting my arm round your waist and whirling you about a ballroom.' He paused to look around him. 'One person looks very happy and it is your little sister, Sarah.'

'Oh dear,' she said, then gave herself to the dance.

It was indeed a happy few moments for those couples who were waltzing.

Oliver, in particular, dancing with an entranced Marianne, felt an exhilarating sense of freedom. James had taught Marianne the waltz and she was a good little dancer; light on her feet and lifting her head to look at her partner as though she had no need to concentrate on the steps. When the music stopped, he kept his arm around the young girl's waist and led her slowly back to her place.

'I could waltz with you all night, Marianne.'

'I do not think Hester would approve. She is looking daggers at me as it is because you still have your arm around my waist.'

'I like it,' he replied with a smile. 'And I shall keep it there until we reach your chair. I am afraid that there are times when Hester can be very forbidding. She is most respectable, you know.'

'Meaning that I am not!' she quipped.

'No, you little puss. I don't mean that at all. You are the most lovely girl here tonight and I was proud to stand up with you. I will have to take Hester into supper, but will you save the second waltz for me, Marianne?'

'I will think about it,' she said, as lightly as she could, for she was aware of feelings in her heart that should not and could not be there.

'Hussy,' he said, and they reached Hester and Bertram. 'Do you not think that Marianne is a fine dancer, Hester? She is going to save the second waltz for me if you do not object. And now I must take you into supper, my dear, I believe the food to be uncommonly good here.' He turned to Marianne. 'Do come with us, Marianne, and you can eat as many of those Chantillies as you like.'

Marianne looked at Hester and, seeing her expression, told the lie. 'Thank you, Oliver, but I have already said that I will go into supper with Philip.'

It was a different story with Sarah and Julian. Sarah was both breathless and happy after her waltz with Julian and it was a shock to her as they reached their chairs to find Philip looking at her fixedly and with an expression which could only be described as bitterly jealous. While Julian was speaking to Anita, Philip took Sarah's arm and drew her to one side.

'Sarah,' he said heatedly, 'I could not bear to see you in Cleeve's arms. I did not know how much you meant to me. Cry off, Sarah, cry off from your betrothal and marry me.'

His grip was on both her hands and she could feel the strength and urgency of his entreaty, but she found herself almost lost for words.

'Philip,' she faltered, 'what are you saying? You will make me embarrassed in front of all these people.'

'What else can I do? I cannot see you on your own now that you are committed to Cleeve. And I care for you so much, my sweet little Sarah.'

His words gave Sarah the clue to what her next words must be. 'Philip, that is just what I have always been ever since we were children together. And you have got some maggot in your brain about Julian. I cannot cry off now, Philip, we have already arranged our marriage – it will be as soon as the year of Julian's mourning for his wife is over. Forget me, Philip; there are many lovely ladies here tonight who must be longing to be asked to dance with you.'

He spoke impatiently. 'How can I forget when you are so beautiful and you hold such a place in my heart? I have clung to the memory of Clara all this time, and it has taken Cleeve's coming to make me realize that you are here for me . . . tell me that I have not left it too late.'

But Sarah knew that, although she felt an unexpected flutter at his words, a public ballroom was no place to say such things. She must get Philip back into a reasonable frame of mind and she tried to speak sensibly.

'Julian is going to dance the second waltz with Anita, so why don't you ask me for that?'

The old Philip suddenly came back though somewhat shamefaced. 'You would give me a waltz when I have behaved so wretchedly to you? I do not deserve such kindness. Forgive me, Sarah, forgive me and dance the waltz with me. I will have you in my arms and we will pretend we are lovers.'

It was said in such a tone of self-mockery that Sarah laughed aloud. 'Whatever will you say next? There is no understanding you.'

'I will tell you once again that I will not give up hope,' he replied, and lifted her hand to his lips. Then he looked round for Marianne and they all went into supper together.

The evening went by all too quickly for the young people and, thinking about it afterwards, the thing that stood out most in Sarah's memory was not the various arguments and changing of partners, but her waltz with Philip.

When the dance was announced, Philip came up to her quite correctly. 'Sarah, my dear, my hand for the waltz?' he said with a gentlemanly courtesy which made her smile. This was far from being the young Philip who had climbed trees with her when she was a tomboyish ten-year-old and he just growing up to be a young man of the world and not yet married to Clara.

'Thank you, Philip,' she smiled.

One hand in hers and the other round her waist, he guided her on to the ballroom floor. Sarah had enjoyed the flourish of dancing with Julian, but with Philip there was a dreamy sensuality to his hold and in his eyes which seemed to speak of love. She let herself fall into his mood and they danced silently until the last bars of the music were played and she found herself standing with him in the shadow of one of the arches that led to the gaming and refreshment rooms.

She did not move, but looked up at him and she caught her breath at his expression. Childhood fell away and she felt the force of a love suddenly born because she had been claimed by Julian Cleeve.

Philip's lips were close to her ear. 'I want to kiss you, Sarah.'

The words jerked Sarah from her trance and she took a step back, cross with herself for being made to recognize feelings that were forbidden to her; and also cross with Philip for arousing those feelings in the first place.

'Philip, we are in a public place and you have no right to speak in such a fashion. Kindly take me back to my chair.'

Philip, knowing he had overstepped the borders of correct behaviour, apologized with his old boyish charm.

'Sorry, Sarah, my sweet, I keep forgetting that you are the property of Mr Julian Cleeve. I will take you back to him and claim my kiss on another occasion.'

'No, you will not, if you please, Philip,' she chided.

'I will consider it, Sarah. Ah, they are just forming for the quadrille. Let us join them.'

'I think I am promised to Julian.' The words somehow lacked enthusiasm and Sarah scolded herself.

'I might have known,' Philip said with mock bitterness. 'I will have to surrender you to him.'

As they approached Julian, Sarah could see an unusual air of annoyance in his face. 'Have you finished your flirtation with Hesslewood, Sarah?' he demanded abruptly.

Sarah felt Philip's hand on her arm grip tightly.

'Perhaps you would like to withdraw that statement, Cleeve.' Philip spoke his words through lips taut with anger.

'I withdraw nothing, but I would remind you that Sarah is betrothed to me.' Sarah had never known Julian so surly in his manner.

'For as long as it suits you, Cleeve.'

Sarah held her breath at Philip's words.

'You dare to insult me at my daughter's come-out?' Julian hissed.

'And how long has she been your daughter?'

'Hesslewood,' Julian took a step forward.

But Philip was gone and Sarah saw him no more that night. She felt both ashamed and mystified by his behaviour and his remarks, but suddenly Julian became all charm.

'Sarah, I am glad you are going to marry me and not that young man. Insolent puppy. Come, they are forming the set for the quadrille.'

Ten

THEY ALL WENT back to London Road from the Assembly Rooms tired and happy, though Sarah found herself haunted by the exchange of words between Philip and Julian. In particular, it was Philip's question to Julian which bothered her. 'And how long has she been your daughter?' he had said.

The more she sought a meaning from the words, the more the mystery of them deepened. Was Philip perhaps hiding something from her that only he knew? Sarah answered herself by remembering that Philip had from the very first meeting with Julian, tried to discredit him in her eyes.

She felt that she could ask neither of the two men if the question had any significance and she decided that the only thing she could do was to try to put it all at the back of her mind. The events of the next morning helped her to do so.

The young people were stirring early and were down to breakfast before anyone else; Jane delighted to have her friends with her, Anita bright and perky, only Marianne seemed quiet. She was not her usual bright self and Sarah was quick to notice it across the breakfast table.

'Marianne, are you quite the thing? I have never known you so quiet.'

Marianne, not wanting to upset her companions, but not feeling at all well, frowned at her sister and tried to pass it off lightly. 'I expect I ate too many creams last night,' she said.

'But your face is flushed,' persisted Sarah.

'Oh no,' replied Marianne. 'I am not in the least hot, in fact I feel quite shivery. Perhaps we are sitting in a draught.'

Sarah got up and walked round the table, putting her hand to Marianne's forehead. 'It is very hot in here,' she said quietly. 'Your forehead is burning; I do believe that you have a fever. Up to bed with you and I will go and speak to Lady Elizabeth. There will be no going back to Cleeve Grange for you today.'

Feeling far from well, Marianne was taken upstairs and Jane's maid came and helped her to undress and get back into bed where she was glad to lie down under warm blankets.

Sarah, not voicing her thoughts but feeling some concern, went in search of Lady Elizabeth. She found her kind hostess in her dressing-room, putting the final touches to her morning toilette.

'Sarah, my dear,' Lady Elizabeth smiled. 'Here I am up so late after such an evening as we had, and I expect that all the girls are already at the breakfast table discussing their success of last night. It was a happy occasion, was it not ... but, Sarah, you look worried. Is something wrong?'

'I do not wish to alarm you, Lady Elizabeth, but I have just put Marianne to bed with a high fever. I am afraid to say that I have heard of cases of scarlet fever in the town. It is a nasty illness and very infectious. What shall I do?'

Lady Elizabeth Humphries had not brought up a large family for nothing. She was a kindly and sensible woman who was not easily flustered.

She stood up and put her hand on Sarah's arm. 'Leave it to me. First of all, I will send a servant for our good Dr Dowdeswell. He is elderly, I know, but he has seen all our children through the various illnesses they fell prey to. Then I will get cook to make some lemonade for Marianne and she must drink as much as she can if she is in a fever.'

'But the infecton, Lady Elizabeth.'

'Do not worry yet, wait and see what the doctor has to say and go and make the arrangements for Sir Bertram to take Lady Hadlow and James back to Little Cleeve as soon as possible.'

There followed a confused hour. The word quickly went round that Marianne had the scarlet fever which they all knew to be both dangerous and highly infectious.

Hester and Oliver quarrelled; Jane refused to leave her friend or her home; Lady Hadlow had a fit of the vapours to be comforted by Bertram; Philip was missing and Julian tried to take things into his own hands. Sarah herself stayed at Marianne's side and watched with dismay as the young girl cried because her throat was so sore and thrashed about restlessly in her fever.

Dr Dowdeswell was over sixty years of age, but he was a tall man who could only be described as hale and hearty. He examined the patient carefully, shook his head and promised that, no, there were no spots on the tongue and that Marianne was suffering from a bad bout of the influenza and not scarlet fever.

'I will send you a saline draught,' he told Sarah. 'Make sure that she takes it regularly. And bathe her body if she feels too hot; I see that you have some lemonade, but I would also recommend some barley water. Nothing to eat, mind you, except perhaps some chicken broth when the fever abates. Now I must go and see Lady Elizabeth for I think she has a houseful of guests after the girls' come-out ball and we want to avoid them all catching the influenza. It is unlikely at this time of year for an epidemic usually comes in the winter, but we must be cautious.'

Sarah thanked the doctor and, a few minutes later, Lady Elizabeth came and sat with Marianne while Sarah went downstairs to see what arrangements could be made.

Bertram was at his most solicitous, but Sarah could hear that

Oliver and Hester were having an argument; she thought perhaps Hester was worried about the scarlet fever and went over to speak to them.

'I must tell you straight away that it is not scarlet fever but a bad go of the influenza,' she said quietly.

Hester's face was pinched and sharp. 'I must go back to London immediately. I cannot take the risk of catching the influenza for I have a weakness of the chest and my mama would never forgive me if I were to have an infection.'

Sarah's eyes narrowed. Not a word of sympathy or enquiry as to how Marianne was, she thought, and looked at Oliver.

His face looked strained as though he had been having a harrowing time and Sarah believed that Hester must have been going on in this vein all the while the doctor had been with Marianne.

'Hester,' Oliver said, his patience very sorely tried, 'I am willing to take you back to your mama straight away. But I will not stay in London. I had arranged to be here for a week and I will not desert my family at a time of trouble.'

Hester held her head higher and managed to look very superior. 'Noble sentiments indeed, Oliver, but I thought that my wishes on the matter would have had the more influence on you.' She turned to Sarah. 'In any case, I do not see why Marianne could not be wrapped in blankets and taken home; the journey is not far. She is causing everyone a great deal of trouble.'

Sarah was stunned by this unfeeling remark and could see the effect it had on Oliver. His generous mouth went into a thin line: his eyebrows almost met in a frown.

'Hester' – his tone was icy cold – 'your feelings and remarks do you no credit. I will ask one of the servants to pack your travelling bag; you will be ready in fifteen minutes, if you please. I will drive you to London and then come straight back here to help my mother and to make sure that Marianne is in no danger. Please be as quick as you can.'

Hester left the room without another word and Oliver put his hand on Sarah's arm. 'I am sorry, Sarah, Hester has been very carefully reared and is an only daughter. She does not see things in the same light as we do, coming from larger families.' He paused. 'How is Marianne?'

'Burning hot one minute and shivering the next,' Sarah replied and hoped that she sounded unconcerned.

'Do you think I might sit with her when I return?' he asked quietly.

Sarah gave a small smile. 'It is kind of you, Oliver. I think it is better that I attend her while she is in a fever, but as soon as she is recovering, I think she will be pleased of your company.' She had to say the next words. 'If you think Hester will not mind, of course.'

'Be damned to Hester,' he exploded, and apologized immediately. 'I am sorry, Sarah, I hardly know what I am thinking. I could almost wish that Hester would cry off. I cannot, can I? It is a lady's privilege, curse it.'

Sarah was disturbed by Oliver's mood. It had been clear from the start that they were an ill-assorted pair, but it was diffcult to know what to say for the best.

'It is a difficult time for Hester. She has obviously been coddled – as we would say – all her life and has a great fear of infections and illness. Perhaps she will think differently once she is home in London with her mother and you will see a change of heart in her.' Sarah was watching Oliver's face as she spoke and saw no lightening of his mood.

'I shall not stay long enough in London to see how she goes on. I had rather be back here.' He looked at her and his face was full of a grave concern. 'Sarah, if you took me up, would it be possible to see Marianne for a minute before I go? I would not stay, but I would like her to know that I am thinking of her.'

Sarah did not think that it was quite the thing, but had not the heart to say no. 'Come straight away, but I warn you that she is very restless and flushed; she cannot sleep, poor dear.'

They crept upstairs and into Marianne's room like two naughty children and, as they entered the room, they could see that Lady Elizabeth was shaking some lavender water on to a handkerchief. She looked up and smiled; then, to Sarah's surprise, she gave the handkerchief to Oliver.

'Just bathe her forehead, Oliver, she would like that. She is so hot at the moment, poor little thing.'

Oliver took the handkerchief and bent over the stricken girl; he rubbed it gently on her forehead.

'Marianne,' he whispered.

Her eyes flew open and she knew him. 'Oliver, how very kind. But please do not catch the influenza from me, I would not like you to have it and then pass it on to Hester.'

'Shhh,' he said softly and then turned to his mother. 'Mama, I am taking Hester back to London and I will return here immediately.'

Not a muscle moved in Lady Elizabeth's face, but Sarah sensed that she was pleased with this news. 'Thank you, Oliver. God speed. We will take care of Marianne for you.'

Sarah and Oliver crept out and Sarah returned downstairs thinking over and over again of the strangeness of Lady Elizabeth's remark to Oliver. When she entered the drawing-room, it was to find that Julian had made arrangements with Bertram to take Lady Hadlow back to Little Cleeve together with James; he would take Anita later, leaving Jane and Sarah to nurse Marianne.

They all dispersed to collect their travelling bags and Jane went upstairs to relieve her mother. Sarah found herself on her own with Julian.

She looked at him accusingly. 'You like to have the ordering of things, Cousin.'

He did not deny it. 'I say what is most practicable, that is all. I could see that your mother was heading towards one of her nervous spasms and knew that she would be best cared for by Bertram. Would you disagree, Sarah?'

Sarah sighed. 'There is no arguing with you. I do believe you are forever right and will have your own way about things in the end.'

'You are very docile today, my sweet. Is Marianne's illness bothering you? How poorly is she? Tell me if there is truly cause for alarm. You made light of it in front of the others.'

'No, Julian, there is no real cause for worry. The fever will run its course and Marianne is a strong girl and will soon make a recover.' She looked at him and knew that she could say what was really bothering her. 'It is Oliver I am thinking of. He is coming back from London immediately to be with Marianne. And it is Hester who should be first in his thoughts. I hardly know what to think.'

She found herself pulled into gentle, caring arms and experienced a great sense of comfort. Julian murmured close to her ear. 'Love will find its way, Sarah, and I have things well in hand.'

Sarah pulled herself away and looked up at him with some indignation. 'And what is that supposed to mean, Cousin? First of all you get Crystal away from James, having already succeeded in uniting Mama and Bertram; I am sure you are encouraging a friendship between James and Anita, and now it is Hester and Oliver! Whatever will you think of next?'

'I think I will kiss you.'

'Oh, Julian, it is no time to think of kissing.'

'I will not see you for a few days, my love, so you must send me on my way with a kiss.'

His lips were forceful on hers, but Sarah's mind was distracted and she did not return the kiss.

'Rake,' she muttered, and for some inexplicable reason, she thought of Philip; she missed him for the first time that morning in all the worry over Marianne. She looked up at Julian. 'Do you know where Philip is? I suppose you are the last person I should be asking.'

'I have to tell you, my peagoose, that it is obvious that Philip thinks he cannot be in the same house as me. He was up betimes, according to James, and has gone back to Luttons Park.'

'Oh,' said Sarah in a small voice. 'He will know nothing about Marianne being ill.'

And she left him and the next time she went upstairs to her bedroom, she found a note propped up on her dressing-table.

Sarah, my love

I apologize for bad behaviour at the ball last night. It is better that Cleeve and I are kept apart. Think of me; I will come and see you soon.

Philip

Without thinking of what she was doing, Sarah put the note to her lips; then, shaking her head in exasperation at both Philip and Julian, she went downstairs again in time to see her mother and Bertram off to Little Cleeve.

Marianne was restless all day and Sarah often heard her cry out Hester's name; she has it on her mind, Sarah thought. But the young girl continued like this until it had grown dark and a maid came in to light the candles. Sarah was about to move a candlestick on the dressing-table when she heard the door being opened very quietly.

Thinking it was Lady Elizabeth, Sarah put the candlestick down and went to the door. 'She keeps calling for Hester. I am at a loss to understand . . .' she started to say. 'Oh, Oliver you have come.'

Indeed it was Oliver, seemingly very tired and still wearing his driving coat. 'How is she?' he whispered.

'She keeps repeating Hester's name . . . perhaps if you speak to her, it will put her mind at rest and she will sleep.'

She helped him with his coat and saw him give rather a weary smile. 'I suppose it was madness to try and do London and back in a day, but I was determined to be here before nightfall.'

He sat by the bed and took Marianne's hand in his. 'Marianne, hush, it is Oliver.'

'Hester.' Just the single name from Marianne.

'I have taken Hester back to her mama so stop worrying about her and say you are pleased to see me.'

'Oh, Oliver it is you, is Hester all right?'

'Yes, she is. I will join her as soon as you are better.'

'I do not wish to come between you,' she whispered.

'No, that will not happen. Go to sleep now.'

'Oliver.' Her voice was drowsy and she lay back and was in a deep sleep within minutes.

Sarah smiled at the young man. 'Thank you, Oliver, she will wake up feeling a lot better, I do believe. And you are to get yourself some brandy and something to eat and then have a good night's sleep. I have a feeling that this young lady will be brighter in the morning and will be pleased to see you.'

Dr Dowdeswell was pleased with his patient next morning and Marianne was soon sitting up in bed and looking pretty in a Kashmir shawl which Lady Elizabeth had found for her.

A little later, not just Oliver but Julian arrived at the same time.

Oliver took one look at Marianne and smiled. 'You are looking better, I am so glad. I have brought you some flowers.' And he put a posy of rosebuds on her bed.

'Thank you, Oliver, I am quite spoiled. Perhaps you and Jane could sit with me and let Cousin Julian take Sarah into the garden for some fresh air.'

'Do not tire yourself, young lady,' Julian replied and turned to Sarah. 'You were with Marianne all night, Sarah, now I insist that you take a turn with me.'

Sir Roger did not own a vast amount of land along with his town house, but he had over the years designed and planted an extensive garden at the rear. It was formal and set out in the Italian style with statuary and flowering shrubs. At the end was a small orchard with a wall for peaches and a stone seat had been placed in a warm and sheltered spot.

Julian had discovered the seat and led Sarah to it now. She felt very pleased to be out in the fresh air after the hot and stuffy atmosphere of the sick-room.

'Is that better, Sarah?' he asked her.

'Yes, thank you, it is, but I must tell you I am not best pleased.'

'And what is worrying that wise little head of yours?'

She turned to look at him and, as always, was struck by his careless elegance, the strength of him beneath the perfect cut of his morning coat. His waistcoat was unexceptional and his neck-cloth casually arranged, but even so he managed to achieve the appearance of any London Corinthian.

'It is everything,' she replied at last.

'Are you worrying about Marianne? I thought she seemed much improved, I am sure you have no need to be in a fidget over her.'

She snapped at his casual manner. 'It is not her health that worries me, it is her obvious liking for Oliver.'

'Oliver?' Julian said as though surprised. 'But I thought the two of them made rather a nice pair.'

Sarah jumped and stood before him in anger. 'If that is not just like you, Julian Cleeve. Being pleased because they seem to like each other, and saying that they would suit. How can you say such things when Oliver is already betrothed to Hester . . . no, do not interrupt. I know that Hester went home at the first sign of influenza in the house, but that has nothing to do with the matter.' Sarah drew breath and found her hands taken into Julian's until she was forced to sit on the seat again.

'It is Oliver I do not understand. How can he make such a fuss over Marianne as he is doing if he is already committed to marrying Hester? Maybe they do suit but you must know it cannot be. And I am afraid all this attention she is getting and rosebuds, if you please – will break her heart. It is wrong of him and I am sorry if I lost my temper but I am at my wits' end. I cannot stop Oliver from seeeing Marianne, but where is it all going to lead?'

'My Sarah, do not be such a goosecap, and try and trust me,' Julian said softly and seriously.

'Trust you when you are doing your best to throw the two of them together? Why, Julian? Why are you doing it?'

He held her hands tightly. 'I am of the opinion that Oliver regrets his betrothal to Hester Brewer and that he has fallen in love with Marianne. I am very fond of Marianne and I sincerely believe that she has met her match in Oliver; the Humphries have always been accquainted with the Wintersons and it is only the accident of the difference in their ages that they have not come across one another before . . . are you listening?'

Sarah nodded but she had to object. 'But, Julian, that does not make his behaviour any the more correct.'

'Think, my little widgeon, think. . . .'

'I am not your anything yet – well, I suppose we are betrothed – but I am certainly not a widgeon. I may be plain and unfashionable but I am not a simpleton.'

'You are beautiful,' he replied.

'Fiddlesticks, you are only saying that to try and placate me when you know very well I am angry.' Sarah's expression was still stormy.

'Sarah, just try and follow what I am going to say to you and then tell me if it makes sense.'

'Very well,' she said flatly.

'It is something Oliver told me this morning. He is quite disenchanted with Hester. It seems that Mrs Brewer opposed the match from the start thinking that plain Mr Humphries was not good enough for her daughter – it should be a baronet, at least. As for Hester herself, she only accepted Oliver's hand because she was at her last prayers, as you say over here, and because it pleased her father that she should marry someone within the legal profession.'

'But, Julian,' Sarah had to interrupt, 'I do see all that, but it does not make Oliver's conduct any the more proper. And what can you do about it?'

'I am biding my time. If he and Marianne enjoy a light flirtation while Oliver is here at home, no harm will be done, because Oliver is a gentleman and will abide by a gentleman's code. In the meantime, Mama Brewer will be producing elderly suitors of some means and Hester will cry off. Then Marianne and Oliver will have fallen in love and you have the makings of a fine romance.'

Sarah looked at him. His expression was wickedly mischievous, but it was also convincing and she gave a laugh. 'Julian, you are devious, there is no other word. But in a way, I hope you are right for I, too, would like to see the young pair together. So it will be a question of "wait and see" and I will have to be satisfied with that. Whatever will you be up to next? I am sure I have asked that question of you before.'

'A secret, Sarah, a secret of my very own. Now give me a kiss and we will go back and sit with Marianne.'

The next few days passed very quickly and very pleasantly, for as soon as she was allowed up, Marianne became her old bright self again.

Sarah found that she could not fault Oliver's behaviour. He always made sure that Jane was there when he was with Marianne and the three of them could often be heard laughing together.

Then came the last day of Oliver's visit and the day that Sarah hoped to take Marianne home to Little Cleeve.

Late morning found Oliver walking in the garden with

Marianne and making a difficult farewell.

Marianne was greatly recovered and enjoyed being out in the fresh air again. But she was subdued in her manner and her words sounded stiff.

'You will be glad to be back in London, Oliver.'

'Yes, I suppose so.'

'You do not sound very sure,' she said.

He turned to her; they were in the shade of a row of lime trees which Sir Roger had planted at the bottom of his formal garden.

'It is true I am not sure. I am not sure of anything since I met you and that is barely a week ago. Can you believe that? I feel as though I have known you forever. I cannot say more than that, Marianne, and you know why, don't you?'

Marianne felt that she could not even smile. 'You are betrothed to Hester, Oliver, and I wish you happy. I did not like being the cause of a quarrel between you so I hope you find that all is well when you return to London.'

Oliver took her by the hand and she did not pull away. 'Thank you. I cannot know what I am going to find. But I want to wish you happy, too, Marianne. You are so lovely, I am certain that you will be all the rage when you go to Brighton. Think of me when you dance the waltz, my dear.'

The thought of the waltz was too much for Marianne. She was weakened by her illness and the thought of parting from Oliver. She felt a tear trickle down her cheek as she stood staring up at him.

With gentle fingers, he wiped her wet face. 'I would like to kiss the tears away, Marianne, but it is forbidden to me. Let us walk back to the house and think of something more cheerful than our parting. When do you go to Brighton?'

Marianne was grateful for the question and his care at turning the conversation away from themselves.

'I think it is sometime next week. Bertram kindly rents a house for us all. Then, when we return from Brighton, there will be Mama's wedding to think about – it is rather strange to think of one's mama having a wedding. It will be very quiet, of course, but I am so pleased for her.'

They looked at each other with nothing else they could say; then, hardly realizing what she was doing, Marianne stood on tiptoe, reached up, and kissed his cheek. 'Thank you for looking after me when I was ill, Oliver. Goodbye.'

'Marianne . . .' he started to say but she was gone.

Later that day, the preparations were made for Sarah and Marianne to return home. James came in the carriage to fetch them and there was much excitement when they arrived at Little Cleeve.

Anita was there with her father and could not wait to tell them that she had been riding with James.

They were all in the drawing-room and Sarah searched for Julian's eyes to see if he was pleased. He came and took her aside into the window embrasure and she was able to speak quietly amidst all the hubbub.

'Julian, are you pleased? About Anita riding again, I mean,' and she watched his face, but his expression gave nothing away.

'I am very pleased, my lovely goose-cap,' he replied.

'I am neither lovely nor a goose-cap. I could write a book of all the names you choose to call me.' She said it seriously, but he knew she was funning.

'I could call you "my love" but love hardly enters our intentions, does it? You will marry me, won't you, Sarah? You will not run off with the jealous Philip?'

'I will have nothing said about Philip, if you please. I thought at one time that he might do for Marianne but then Oliver Humphries arrived on the scene. I know I was cross that you encouraged them, but he has behaved impeccably; they said goodbye this morning and he has gone back to Hester. I must say that Marianne is putting on a very brave face. I think she is pleased to be with Anita again and now they will be able to ride together.'

Julian was silent and, getting no reply, Sarah spoke to him again. 'Were you listening, Julian?'

'Yes, my sweet, I was. I was trying to think of something I could do about Hester,' he said slowly.

Sarah was alarmed. 'Julian, you cannot interfere. It is up to Hester to cry off.'

'Yes, I know that,' he replied. 'I will have to think about it. When do you go to Brighton, Sarah?'

'About the first week in August. Are you going to try for a house for you and Anita, Julian?'

'No, Sarah, I am not. I hope you will excuse me; I have business in London and I plan to take Anita with me. Does Philip go?'

'For a few days, yes,' she told him.

'Can I leave you with him, or is it asking for trouble? He is very possessive about you.'

'He will behave quite properly, I am sure,' Sarah said rather primly.

'I am not so sure, but I trust you.'

'Thank you, Julian, I shall miss you.'

'That is nicely said, my sweet Sarah. I will bid you goodbye for a few weeks.' And he bent and touched her lips with his, but Sarah thought the kiss both perfunctory and absent-minded, as though Julian had something else on his mind.

He turned to Anita and Marianne. 'Come along, young rascals, it is time to be going back to the Grange.'

That evening, Sarah found herself worrying about Marianne and decided to walk up to Cleeve Grange and make sure that her sister was settled in once again.

It was a warm evening, and Sarah, still dressed in her afternoon gown of a creamy sarsenet carried only a Norwich shawl about her arms.

She let herself in at the front entrance hall without announcing herself. From the direction of the kitchen came a murmur of voices. She stopped, thinking that she would have a quick chat with Mrs Lingfield before going in search of Marianne.

At the kitchen door, she did not recognize the voices until one was raised and she knew it was Anita.

'But, John, what will we do if he comes here. . . ?'

Then silence as though the speaker had been stopped and in her imagination, Sarah could picture that the two were embracing.

Hot with embarrassment, she walked quietly to the drawing-room. What was Anita up to, she was thinking furiously? Surely she is not indulging in a friendship with John Capel? John was a tall man of a rugged and handsome type, accustomed by his duties as steward, to being out of doors in all weathers, just like Philip. But although she knew him to be a bachelor, he was nearer in age to Julian and surely would not press his attentions on the young Anita? The thoughts had come to Sarah and gone in a flash as she opened the drawing-room door, saying to herself – don't be so foolish, Sarah.

She found Marianne at the pianoforte and quite alone.

'How are you feeling, Marianne?' Sarah said cheerfully. 'And where is Anita?'

Marianne got down from the piano stool. 'It is lovely to be back again, Sarah. Lady Elizabeth and Jane were so very kind, but it was a worrying time.'

Sarah knew that her sister was referring to Oliver and did not press the matter; she asked her question again. 'What has happened to Anita?'

'I think she has gone for a short ride with Cousin Julian. She is so pleased James persuaded her to ride again. I think she wanted to show off her skills.'

If Sarah had misgivings, she did not show them, but she was

sure that it had been Anita's voice coming from the kitchen. And if John Capel was taken up with Anita, she must forget about it.

She stayed an hour with Marianne and Anita came in her usual bright self, pleased to have her companion back again.

Sarah walked back to Little Cleeve feeling pulled between Julian's kindness and Philip's assertion that all was not what it seemed. I am being fanciful, she told herself; Marianne is safely home and if Julian can work some magic to secure Oliver for her sister, she would be eternally grateful to him.

Eleven

PHILIP WAS THE first to arrive at Little Cleeve the following morning and Sarah found herself pleased to see him. He rode up with his brother and, as Bertram immediately settled himself with Lady Hadlow in the drawing-room, Sarah suggested a walk in the garden.

As they strolled through the shrubbery, she was remembering the last time she had been there with Philip and jokingly made a reference to it.

'Best behaviour this time, Philip.'

'Always with you, Sarah,' he replied with a smile. 'It is only Cleeve who brings out a demon in me.'

'Then you will be pleased to hear that he and Anita do not propose to come to Brighton with us. He intends to take her on a trip to London, though what there is to do in London in August, I cannot imagine. But you will come to Brighton, Philip?' she asked him.

'For a few days perhaps. It is a great occasion for my brother.'

Sarah nodded. 'I know how keen Bertram is to be there when the Regent is in residence. Bertram seems to count him as one of his cronies though I am not sure why – unless it is because they are both so fat. . . .'

Philip burst into laughter. 'Sarah, you are disrespectful! How can you speak of my brother in such a fashion? It is not so long ago that you were seriously contemplating his offer of marriage. As for the Regent, I fail to understand what he can have in common with Bertram.'

Sarah gave some thought to the matter. 'The Regent, for all his excesses, is known to be a generous patron of the arts; that must be where they share the same interests. You know what a fine collection of paintings and porcelain Bertram has at Luttons Park.'

Philip deftly turned the conversation to themselves. 'I will be able to enjoy having you to myself in Brighton then, Sarah, that will be very pleasant,' he said quietly, and she looked up and met his eyes which held an expression that was quite disquieting.

'I choose not to hear that remark,' she returned swiftly. 'You are becoming a dangerous companion, Philip.'

'Good, I will continue in my efforts to steal you from the all-powerful Mr Cleeve.'

'I cannot take you seriously, though I suppose I am being greedy. I want to marry Julian and live at Cleeve Grange, yet I do not wish to lose our friendship, Philip; neither do I want any scenes like the one at the ball. I think I had better contrive to keep the two of you apart or I shall have trouble on my hands.'

'I promise not to embarrass you, Sarah,' said Philip and she thought he had spoken with every good intention. 'You look charming this morning. Why did I never realize how beautiful you are?'

Sarah laughed. 'That is an easy question to answer. It is because I am not beautiful. My looks are very ordinary; Marianne is the beauty in our family.'

'No, I disagree,' he said. 'Marianne is certainly very pretty, but she does not possess your poise and grace.'

'Doing it too brown, Philip. Are you out to flatter me because Julian is not here?' Sarah kept her tone light, she was not prepared to be drawn into an argument with Philip. She was committed to Julian, but when she was with Philip, she was assailed with doubts about her own true feelings. It was not until she was with Julian again that she would feel she had been right to accept his offer. In a way, she felt pulled and tugged in two directions and it did not give for peace of mind.

'I am not going to argue today,' he said easily. 'I am going to enjoy having you to myself for a short while.'

They were standing close and Sarah looked up into his eyes to see if he was serious. She found him to be smiling at her as he took her hands in his. 'Give me your hands,' he said, 'and we will sit at the end of the garden and have a civilized conversation.'

Sarah gave a quiet and happy laugh and it was on this scene that Julian Cleeve arrived.

'Sarah.' His voice was as thunder.

Sarah snatched her hands from Philip's grasp and spun herself round to see a Julian whose look was as thunderous as his voice; his mouth drawn in a straight line, his grey eyes with an icy, hostile expression.

He walked towards them still scowling and Philip, without thinking, put his hand to Sarah's shoulder as though to protect her. Sarah herself felt cold and stiff with embarrassment and guilt and she could not say a word.

It was Julian who spoke; short, clipped, hard words. 'So this is what goes on when I am not here. You did not expect to see me today, Sarah. Did you flee to your lover the moment you had said goodbye to me and thought me safely in London?'

Philip pushed Sarah behind him and she could feel the rage in his body. But she was unable to take her eyes from Julian; she wanted to run into his arms and beg him not to look so ferocious.

She had reckoned without Philip. His tone, like Julian's, was icy.

'Sarah is like a sister to me, Cleeve, and you will take back those words. If I could, I would prevent her from marrying a man who is beneath her in moral behaviour and is certainly no gentleman.'

Julian was now tall and rigid with a murderous fury. 'I take that as an insult, Hesslewood, withdraw your words immediately.'

'I withdraw nothing. You are no more than a libertine and a scoundrel.' Philip's words were loud and clear in the quiet garden.

'I demand satisfaction,' were the curt words from Julian. 'Name your second and ask him to call on John Capel.'

Philip was tense. 'James will act for me and it will be pistols. . . .'

Sarah screamed. She did not know she had screamed, but she heard the cry rending the air as she threw herself at Julian.

'You cannot fight . . . you cannot fight over me, don't be such fools. It is as Philip says, Julian, he is as a brother to me . . . Philip, withdraw your words, you cannot fight a duel over me . . . Philip please. . . .' But Sarah was talking into the air for Philip had quickly left the garden.

She turned back to Julian. 'You cannot fight with pistols; not over a silly thing like finding me in the garden with Philip. Julian, say something . . . you do not really mean to have a duel, do you?'

He did not even look at her and pushed her roughly away from him. 'Hesslewood has insulted me and refused to apologize. It is a matter of honour between gentlemen. I must go and talk to John Capel.'

'Julian . . .' she cried out with a desperate anger, but he was gone.

Sarah never knew how she passed the rest of that day; she hardly spoke to her mother and there was no one she could turn to. She was wishing that James was there, but Philip had named James as his second . . . what does it mean, she kept saying? Why did Philip make such a remark and so deliberately? And why did Julian want satisfaction? They cannot fight, not over me . . . I love them both in different ways. Julian is only defending his good name. Why, Philip, why?

And so her disordered thoughts went on and on. She did

provide herself some relief by riding out on Cilla in the afternoon and in the evening, to her relief, James came to see her.

Once again the garden was the scene of an unhappy situation, for Sarah knew that they could not talk in front of Lady Hadlow.

They sat on the seat and stared at each other; Sarah thought that the worry of the day had made James look older than his years. She threw herself into his arms and he held her tight.

'What shall we do, James, can you stop them?'

James spoke carefully. 'Both John Capel and I have tried to speak with them, it is our duty, but Philip insulted our cousin, Sarah. It is a matter of honour.'

'That is what Julian said.' She hardly dared speak the next words. 'Is it arranged?' she asked hoarsely.

'Dawn tomorrow, Low Reed Meadow, pistols. And I have obtained the services of a sawbones from Tunbridge Wells.'

Sarah shut her eyes; a surgeon was needed for only one reason and she dare not think about that.

'But James, why did Philip speak in such a way?'

'I think he was provoked into it.'

She nodded. 'Yes, it is true. Julian found us holding hands and called us lovers and that is not so. You do know that, James, don't you?'

'Yes, I know it, Sarah, because I know you,' he said quietly. 'They have always detested each other. Philip seems to know something about Julian that neither of us know. And I cannot get him to tell me.'

'I think it is something to do with Anita,' Sarah replied.

James was thoughtful. 'There is something odd. You know I was set on persuading Anita to ride when she was so fearful?'

'Yes,' Sarah nodded.

'Well, I rode over to Cleeve Grange and we went round to the stables. Julian had provided ponies for both Marianne and Anita and also a very fine mare, Holly, very frisky she was. Anita refused to go on the pony and she let me hand her up on to Holly, no trouble at all. And she was off like the wind, just as though she had ridden the mare all her life. I could not catch her even on Turk. Can you understand it?'

She shook her head. 'No. I had thought she had simply lost her nerve after the riding accident. But you know, James, Philip did tell me once that he had seen Julian and Anita out riding very early one morning. I thought he must be mistaken and I said so.'

'You know what I think, Sarah,' James said suddenly.

'Have you thought of a way of stopping the duel?'

'No, they are set on it. But I think Philip will delope. I don't think he really wants Cousin Julian dead.'

'It could be Philip,' she said miserably. 'James, do not think about such an outcome, I am sure I will not sleep, but you will come to me in the morning when it is all over, won't you?'

'Of course.' And he gave her a kiss, went round to the stables for Turk and rode back to Luttons.

Sarah had been right in saying that she would not sleep that night; she tossed and turned; she saw first Julian lying dead and then it would be Philip. In the end, she went downstairs and poured herself some brandy, but it was to no avail. She wondered if she should go to Cleeve Grange and argue it out with Julian, then she would think that it might make more sense to appeal to Philip.

The two men had been opposed almost from the start when Philip had shown his mistrust of the American cousin. But that they should fight over her . . . Sarah felt that she had dreamed the whole affair and tried to settle down, then, roused again by her thoughts, she paced up and down her bedroom and sipped some more brandy.

She did not cry.

As she saw the first light creep round the corner of the curtains, she made up her mind: she would stop the duel.

She acted quickly, losing no time. She put on her riding dress, went quietly down the stairs, out to the stables, saddled Cilla herself and was on the mare's back riding as fast as she could over to Low Reed Meadow.

She knew exactly the spot where the duel was to take place; it was a water meadow alongside the stream which divided the land of Cleeve Grange and Luttons Park. To Sarah it was a place of happy memories for it was here that Philip had brought her to fish for minnows when she was old enough to ride her own pony.

There were never cattle or sheep in this meadow, the grass was rough and tufted, the stream flooded its banks in the winter rains.

Sarah knew that at this hour in July, the mist would rise from the water and hang still over the meadow.

James had said 'at dawn', she was thinking as she neared the meadow, but dawn was an indeterminate hour; it could mean at the rising of the sun, it could mean the half-hour of light before the sun rose.

Sarah kept these pictures in her mind as she tried to quell the images of angry men, smoking pistols and the call of 'Fire'. She knew enough about duels from the novels she had read to give her a terror and yet also a determination.

She had no idea of what exactly she might do, but if it was in her power to stop the duel, she would do so.

She saw the mist suddenly, but all was quiet. It was not quite light and no birds sang. She was in time.

'I cannot do it,' she said out loud with a sense of panic. It is your duty, said another voice. Steady, Cilla, steady, girl, said a third.

And Sarah was there. Off Cilla's back and gently leading her towards the field. She could not understand the silence, and braced herself to finding a fallen body, the surgeon perhaps doing his job.

She stopped under a tree puzzled, for by now the whole width of the meadow was in her sights. Nothing stirred, the mist drifted slowly away from the water, the trees along the stream were still, lifeless she thought.

Then her eye caught sight of the small group and she froze. Philip; James; an elderly gentleman; their horses grazing restlessly by the water's edge where the grass was greenest.

Sarah gripped her hand on Cilla's reins, feeling the leather cutting through her riding gloves. Philip but no Julian? The elderly man – the surgeon? She was too early and she did not know if the realization gave her relief or even more terror.

She calmed herself and looked at the sombre group closely. Philip the tallest, all in black and standing straight and stiff, staring ahead of him. James, also in black, but slighter and less tall, also rigid, his eyes down the meadow. Beside them, the short man in the shabby clothes, a leather bag in his hand. Obviously the surgeon, just as she had thought.

At their feet, a solid wooden box, ominously the duelling pistols which Philip was sure to have fetched from Luttons Park.

Minutes went by and Sarah tried not to move or let herself be seen. She also tried her best not to feel sickly or squeamish for her turn was to come.

Her senses alert, she heard a galloping horse in the distance; in seconds, the horse was riding up to the small group and Sarah cried out. 'Julian, Julian, do not, oh please do not. . . .' She left Cilla, and her voice failed as she ran forward.

At the very same time, Philip called, 'Sarah, for God's sake. . . .' It was as far as she got for by this time, Sarah had stopped. She had seen with a gasp of astonishment that the rider was not Julian Cleeve, but John Capel, his steward and his second.

Sensing that something was wrong, she stayed where she was and watched the proceedings. John Capel spoke to James and then to Philip . . . after a moment's conversation, he put his hand into his pocket and drew out a scrap of paper which he gave to Philip.

Sarah watched Philip and could see him staring intently at the words which had been written to him.

Then a loud 'Ha!' and he walked towards her.

'Philip, what is it? Has something happened to Julian?'

He was now near enough to grip her by the arms and shake her. 'What are you doing here, you little fool?'

'Don't say that, Philip, I was going to try and stop the duel. But you must tell me what has happened.'

'Anita has got the toothache.'

She stared at him and then burst into tears of rage and frustration all at the same time.

He took her in his arms and she sobbed briefly against his chest. 'Don't play with me, Philip, not at a time like this. Has something happened to Julian, why has John Capel come on his own?'

'The man's a coward, Sarah, as well as the other names I called him.'

'Philip.' There was a deep reproach in Sarah's voice.

'Read it for yourself then,' he said and thrust the piece of paper into her hands.

The first rays of the sun were casting an eerie light over the meadow, but Sarah could read the words easily. There were very few and were in a hasty scrawl.

Hesslewood

Anita has been up all night with the toothache and looks to have an abcess. I have taken her to London and will settle our score on my return in a few weeks' time. *Cleeve*

Tears sprang to Sarah's eyes again. 'Oh, I am so glad, Philip. . . .' Then she stopped at the look of scorn in his eyes. 'Oh I suppose it is this honour thing again. I am sure that you will apologize to Julian in the end.'

'A woman can never understand, Sarah my love. Let me pay off the sawbones, then James and I will take you back to the dower house for some breakfast. Then you can go home at a decent hour and pretend to Lady Hadlow that you got up for an early ride.'

Sanity suddenly came to Sarah as she listened to the voice of a Philip who was not the person who had taken such a violent dislike to Julian Cleeve.

So she said very quietly, 'Thank you, Philip. I would like that.'

She saw the surgeon and John Capel ride off in the direction of Cleeve Grange and looked at the tall, sturdy steward, her mind going back reluctantly to the overheard words of the night before. And she found herself thinking that Anita had shown no signs of the toothache then. . . .

At the dower house, there was a lot of talk and eating and drinking; then before she left, Sarah managed a quiet word with Philip.

They sat on the settle in the breakfast-room and he put his arm around her shoulders in a friendly and comforting gesture.

'I have to say it to you, Sarah, I am sorry for upsetting you, but I am not sorry for what I said to Cleeve for he was casting a slur on your name. Maybe a duel was not necessary, but it is how these affairs are settled honourably and you have to understand this. It was Cleeve's intention to take Anita to London in any case, so a few days makes little difference – I have my doubts about the toothache though. He would have realized that once the affair had got abroad, it would have been your reputation that would have been soiled. It is quite true that if you are betrothed to one man then you should not be seen holding hands with another. I called Cleeve a coward but if he chose this way out in order to save your good name then I must be grateful to him. Do you understand all that?'

She nodded. 'Yes, I do, Philip, thank you. I think it has ended honourably even without a duel being fought.'

'You should not have come out this morning, my sweet.'

Sarah's old spirit returned to her. 'You could hardly expect me to stay at home and let the two of you kill each other, could you? The two gentlemen I love best in all the world!'

Philip kissed her cheek. 'One day you will be able to decide which one you love the best,' he said, as though it was his final word. 'James will ride home with you and I will come to see you in Brighton in a little while.'

'I shall be looking forward to your visit. I shall expect you to be on your best behaviour.'

'Without a doubt, Sarah,' he laughed.

Feeling restored, Sarah rode back to Little Cleeve with James. They had some toast and tea with their mother then James suggested that Sarah should go to Cleeve Grange in the carriage and bring Marianne home. She would be sure to have a lot of dresses and gowns to take to Brighton with her, he said.

'And, Sarah,' he said as he kissed her goodbye, 'don't get involved in any more duels.'

'I promise, James, and thank you for helping Philip.'

At Cleeve Grange, Sarah found Marianne in a worry. She ran out to greet Sarah when she saw the carriage and gave her sister a hug.

'I am so glad you have come, Sarah, for I do not seem to understand anything. Come into the drawing-room and I will tell you the whole. Late last night, Anita complained of the toothache so Mrs Lingfield found a small piece of camphor for Anita to keep in her mouth to help the pain and she went to bed early. But I think she can't have slept for I heard her moving about her room and talking very quietly to Cousin Julian. I went in once to ask her if she was all right and she was quite sharp with me and just said "Yes, thank you, leave me alone". So I went out again, but I had noticed that there was a big valise on the bed and she was putting dresses into it and she did not complain of her tooth hurting at all.

'I went to sleep again and when I went down to breakfast, Mrs

Stockdale said, "Such a thing, the master has taken Miss Anita to London to have a tooth drawn. And she has left you a note, Miss Marianne, and there is another one on the hall table addressed to Miss Sarah in the master's hand".

'Well, I opened my note and all it said was "Papa has taken me to London to have a tooth drawn. We will be gone a little while so you can go home to Little Cleeve if you wish to. Love, Anita".

'And that is all, Sarah, shall I fetch your note for you?'

Sarah had determined to say nothing to anybody about the duel and neither did she tell Marianne that she was dubious about the toothache.

So Marianne fetched the note and Sarah read it quietly to herself.

Sarah,

Anita has the wretched toothache and I am taking her to London. We will stay for a few weeks as planned. Enjoy your stay in Brighton, and I hope that Hesslewood will keep his distance and that the miserable affair can be put off until my return, or forgotten altogether. I look forward to being with you for your mama's wedding to Sir Bertram and then we will be able to plan our own.

Julian

Sarah gave it to Marianne to read and prepared herself for her sister's question.

'What does he mean by "the miserable affair"?' asked Marianne.

'Oh, it was just a quarrel between Julian and Philip; it will soon be forgotten,' said Sarah cheerfully and helped Marianne to pack all she would need for the visit to Brighton.

Sarah was glad of those few busy days of packing and preparation for their holiday as it helped her to forget the startling events of that day at Low Reed Meadow. With Julian gone and Philip careful not to visit, she could concentrate quietly on what was necessary for their stay in Brighton.

The journey to Brighton was easily made in the Little Cleeve and Luttons carriages, carrying Bertram and Lady Hadlow in one and Sarah and Marianne in the other. Bertram had secured the usual spacious house on the Steyne with its drawing-room on the first floor. This always amused the families who were accustomed to large country houses with the reception room downstairs. There was room in the stables for both carriages and Philip's curricle when he arrived; he had promised to join them, leaving James in charge at Luttons Park.

The Humphries had taken a small house just off the Marine Parade so that Jane would be close to Marianne, and this pleased Sarah. Oliver had said that he would bring Hester later in the month, but this last piece of news did nothing to cheer the young people although it did not succeed in dampening their spirits.

Once settled, Lady Hadlow often walked with Bertram on the Steyne as that was the fashionable thing to do, Sarah sometimes accompanying them. The Marine Pavilion always astonished her: built in the previous century for the Prince of Wales, it was designed in the classical style and was a long, low building which would have been imposing had it not been for the domed rotunda which gave it an eastern appearance.

'It looks rather strange amongst all the formal styles of the Brighton town houses,' remarked Sarah to Bertram who knew all about it and repeated it at length.

'The Regent is planning to redesign his pavilion,' he told Sarah. 'Or I should correctly say that the architect John Nash is rebuilding it for him – the same Nash who designed Regent Street in London, you know, quite classical. I have heard that it is to be completely in the Eastern style and will be quite unusual. The Prince is of an artistic mind and is also musical, attributes which are often forgotten in the scandals surrounding his name. I must tell you, Sarah, that we have an invitation to an evening party to be given by him.'

Sarah was wont to think that it was conversations such as these that made her appreciate Julian and all he had done for them; her mama was certainly happier with Sir Bertram than she would have been.

The evening party pleased Marianne and Jane who talked of nothing else for days. Marianne had regained her high spirits, though sometimes Sarah would catch her with a dreamy, rather sad, faraway look in her eyes, when she knew her sister to be thinking of Oliver Humphries.

By the time the day arrived for the Regent's party, Philip had joined them and Sarah found herself pleased to have his company.

The great evening came, and all the best gowns were brought out. Sarah looked particularly charming in a heavy silk of soft blue, but she was almost put in the shade by her mama who looked quite the mature beauty she was, dressed in pale gold. Her gown was by now, old-fashioned, but the sense of the occasion had lifted her often fragile spirits. She walked into the room where they were to be received by the Regent as though she was a queen. She was on Bertram's arm followed by Marianne and Jane, and Sarah with Philip.

Sarah was looking round her in astonishment for she had never before seen such exotic extravagance and colour. The walls were gilded and the room was brilliantly lit, gold and yellow seeming to be the dominant colours. She knew of the Regent's taste for Oriental art, but had not expected it to be so much in abundance in a room which was only a reception room. She found it all completely overwhelming.

Then she heard a whisper in her ear. 'Hideous, is it not?'

Her eyes looked into Philip's expecting to find laughter, but discovered him to be quite serious.

'It is not to my taste . . .' she began. 'Hush, Philip, we are about to be presented.'

Sarah had not known what to expect of the Prince Regent. He had lived a dissolute life and she expected it to have aged him; but at fifty-four, there was no sign of debauchery in his features. He still possessed the charm and ease of manner of his youth and showed it to all those presented to him.

Sarah was amused as Bertram stepped up to him and presented her mama, for the two men, so alike in stature – both being tall and corpulent – were totally dissimilar in looks and manner, the Regent's rather handsome features contrasting oddly with the ruddy, outdoor complexion of Bertram.

'Ha, Hesslewood, pleased to meet you again. Must show you my latest piece of Satsuma ware, a dish of enamelled yellow and gold, the colours not unlike this room. I incline to the East these days, as you know . . . and your companion is Lady Hadlow. You are recently betrothed? So pleased, dear lady, and wearing gold, too, very beautiful . . . sorry about Hadlow, a good gaming fellow always. I cannot believe it is four years since he left us. And these are your charming daughters. . . ?'

And so he went on to each person presented to him and for the time they were in his presence, his amiable pleasantries and lack of formality made each and everyone forget his bad name and give themselves up to the enjoyment of the evening.

The happy events of that evening spent at the pavilion were rapidly eclipsed by the happenings of the following day.

They were all inclined to a late breakfast with Philip and Sarah trying to decide what to do with the day. Philip suggested a trip to Lewes, perhaps taking Marianne with them if she would like to go.

But Marianne was shaking her head. 'No, I do not think I will come with you,' she replied quietly. 'I will be quite happy to walk along the Steyne with Mama and Bertram. It will be nice for you to have an outing on your own.'

'Well said, Marianne,' said Philip, and he turned to Sarah. 'You will come, Sarah?'

But Sarah was hesitating for she knew that Marianne was not aware of the circumstances of the quarrel. 'I am not sure that it is correct for us to be seen together, Philip.'

'It is not correct if you are thinking of Julian. But I don't think even your cousin would object to a curricle trip in Brighton on a fine summer's day. It will be very proper.'

'If you say so, Philip. I must admit to liking the idea. I will fetch my pelisse and bonnet.'

When she joined Philip at the front door, she found him in a playful mood.

'A whole day to ourselves, Sarah, we will pretend we are sweethearts.'

'We will do nothing of the kind,' she said, instantly cross. 'And I will not come if you are in that kind of mood; I do not want another duel on my hands.'

'I promise best behaviour,' smiled Philip.

'And so I should think,' she returned.

He continued to look at her. 'Sarah, do you have to wear that bonnet? I cannot see your face.'

'Of course I must wear a bonnet,' she said, still cross. 'I cannot be seen out of doors without one. You must know that.'

He sighed. 'I suppose so, you can take it off when we have a nuncheon.'

She glanced up at him. 'Are we going to have a nuncheon? I thought it was a morning drive into the country.'

'No, it is our day. I have stolen you from Julian for a day and if I get into trouble with him, it will have been worthwhile.'

So Sarah smiled and threw off her doubts as to the propriety of the trip; she could not resist a Philip in this kind of mood.

It was to be a day of fun and laughter, of light badinage, of friendship and, as they returned to Brighton in the late afternoon, Sarah was quiet and pensive.

Sometimes I wish it was Philip I was going to marry, she said to herself while he concentrated on weaving in and out of the carriages and carts on the way back to Brighton. I do not seem to know my own mind yet I really have no choice. When Julian made his offer, Philip was beyond reach, still wedded to the past. I know I am very drawn to Julian, but is it love? I cannot even answer my own question, so things must stay as they are.

But Philip, although he was concentrating on his reins, was quick to sense her mood and he, too, had his inward thoughts.

I love Sarah, he told himself, it has taken me all this time to forget Clara and now it is too late. I am a fool.

Instead of going straight to the house on the Steyne, he stopped the curricle for a moment within sight and sound of the sea.

Sarah glanced up at him with a little frown but did not speak.

'End of a perfect day, Sarah, now we are home. Will you let me have a kiss?'

'Certainly not,' came her quick reply. 'Julian would be challenging you again and you cannot kiss me amongst all these people on the promenade in Brighton.'

'No one will see,' he murmured, taking no notice of her words and leaning towards her. 'Your bonnet has its uses after all!'

'No, you cannot . . . oh, Philip.'

For his lips were on hers and she did not, could not, pull away. She did not want to – oh, Philip, her heart said.

A minute later, he was driving through the streets as though nothing had happened and they returned to the house on the Steyne to find that a drama had unfolded in their absence.

In the middle of that afternoon, Jane having returned to the Humphries' house, Marianne found herself alone in the drawing-room with nothing but her book and her needlework to occupy her mind. Even her mama was missing having walked to the circulating library with Bertram.

Their departure set Marianne thinking. Not of Oliver, for those thoughts were too painful and brought ready tears, but of those closest and dearest to her, being her mother and Sarah.

It gave her great comfort to know that her mama and Bertram had been brought together for she knew that Lady Hadlow would delight in being at Luttons Park.

Of Sarah, she was not so sure. Sarah and Cousin Julian are often at odds and it sometimes seems an unsuitable match, but perhaps she loves him, she was thinking. Yet I have to feel sorry that it is not Philip who is going to be my brother-in-law. I am sure he is at last forgetting his grief over Clara and has come to love Sarah. Alas, it is too late. . . .

Her thoughts were interrupted by a loud knocking at the front door and when the maid let the visitor in, Marianne thought she heard a man's voice. She stiffened, for it was a voice which made her gasp and her heart stand still.

A minute later, there were steps on the stairs. Nancy opened the door and Oliver was in the room.

'Marianne,' he burst out with obvious excitement. 'Have I been lucky enough to find you on your own? Where is your mama?'

Marianne faltered. The beloved face was in front of her, his hands were holding hers very tightly. 'Oliver, I do not wish to see you. Please understand, it is too painful. . . . Mama has gone out with Bertram, and Sarah has driven to Lewes with Philip.'

'I don't care where they are. In fact, I am glad they are not here for I have some news which is for your ears alone and I am not going to wait until you are chaperoned. We know each other well enough to disregard that nicety.' He was dressed in a riding coat with many capes and he took it off and threw it on a chair. Marianne was in her usual blue, a sprigged muslin which suited both the warm day and her fair curls.

'Please excuse my dirt,' he went on. 'I have been driving my curricle from London since first thing this morning, I could not get here fast enough. You look lovely, Marianne; you must always wear blue.'

By now, Marianne was staring at him in fascination, she had almost forgotten how tall and handsome he was, and he was smiling so happily. But she was forced to ask her question.

'Have you brought Hester with you, Oliver?'

'No more Hester,' was all he said in reply.

Marianne could not help her stammer. 'Wh-what do you mean? Whatever are you saying?'

'Hester has cried off, met an earl, or a marquis, or something. She does not wish to marry me.' Still holding her hands, he pulled her close to him and, in her astonishment, she made no move to resist. 'I had to come and tell you straight away. Did you ever hear such good news? Can I kiss you to celebrate?'

But Oliver was in no mood to wait for a reply. He bent down and his lips found hers and the two of them were lost to the world. Marianne felt the magic of the kiss, but then remembered that she was on her own with Oliver and pulled herself away to face him.

'We should not, Oliver, we are quite on our own . . . and, is it true about Hester? Why have you come racing down to Brighton to tell me?'

'Your mama will not mind me stealing one kiss when she hears the good news. I wanted you to be the very first to know. It means I can tell you that I love you and it means that I can ask you to be my wife. Will you marry me, dear Marianne, and come to London to be the wife of a respectable lawyer? I cannot offer you riches, but I can offer you love and a comfortable home . . . what is it, my sweet, am I going too fast for you? I am a brute.' And he kissed her again, just a light touch on the cheek.

'I received a letter from Hester this morning and replied to it immediately before I set off for Brighton. So I have had the whole journey in which to think about it and to think about you. What else can I say?'

'Would you read Hester's letter to me?'

He smiled and sat her on the sofa beside him. 'Of course I will, I have it here. I do not think you will believe me until you have heard the words yourself. Here you are, I will read it to you, it is not very long.'

Dear Oliver

I came to realize on out visit to Tunbridge Wells that we should not suit and have waited for the chance to ask you to release me from our betrothal. An old friend of Mama's has been visiting and has kindly intimated that he will ask for my hand once I am free. He is Lord Cawcliffe, a man of modest means, but with a fine country estate as well as a house in town.

Papa is disappointed but hopes you will continue your good work with him. We may meet occasionally and I trust it can be without embarrassment and that we can remain friends.

Yours sincerely

Hester

Marianne listened to the words with a sense of awe. 'She is very formal, Oliver, did you love her at one time?'

He shook his head. 'Never. I thought it a suitable match because of my regard for her father. But I did not know what love meant until I met you.' He looked at her searchingly. 'Marianne, is it possible that you feel the same for me?'

She reached up and kissed his cheek shyly. 'Yes, I do love you, Oliver, I love you very much. I was heartbroken when you returned to London, but I have tried not to appear too sad for the sake of all the others. . . .' She paused as though listening. 'Someone has come in the front door – oh, what shall we do?'

'Whoever it is will be told our good news,' he replied gladly and kissed her again.

Minutes later, it was a scene of chaos because Lady Hadlow and Bertram had arrived back at the same time as Philip and Sarah.

Marianne flew into her mother's arms. 'Mama, you will never guess. Hester has cried off; she is going to marry a Lord somebody though he is not wealthy and Oliver has asked me to marry him and I have said yes, but I suppose he should have applied to you first. I may marry him? You will be pleased for me won't you?'

Lady Hadlow sat down quite overcome and Bertram had to find the vinaigrette; then Oliver read Hester's letter once more to convince them.

When the excitement had died down and Lady Hadlow had given them her blessing, Oliver insisted on taking Marianne to see his parents.

There were tears in Lady Elizabeth's eyes as she kissed Marianne. 'I welcome you as a daughter with great delight, Marianne. We would have been glad for Oliver to have married Hester as he has the greatest respect for Mr Brewer, but somehow Hester – always though very polite – managed to make us feel we were her inferiors and we were never comfortable with her. As soon as I met you, I found myself naughtily wishing that Oliver had found you first, but now it has all come right.' Marianne thanked her shyly and gave the invitation from Sir Bertram, to join them that evening for a celebratory dinner.

Twelve

SARAH HAD BEEN wishing that Julian had been there to hear of the successful engagement between Oliver and Marianne. It was not until the next morning when she received a long letter from him that she knew the whole truth of the matter. She read the letter in the quiet of her bedroom, almost unable to believe his words. Then she went in search of Philip so that she could share her news with him.

He was talking to Bertram in the drawing-room with a view to them all taking a trip to Worthing in the carriage that afternoon. He turned and smiled at Sarah as she came into the room.

'Philip, I have received a long letter from Julian which is unbelievable. Please walk out with me so that I can tell you the whole and hopefully banish all your doubts about him.'

'What has he been meddling in now, Sarah?' asked Philip, but his tone did not hold any animosity.

'He is not meddling, as you put it. He is kindness itself and I do want to tell you.' She turned to Bertram. 'I expect you will be walking out with Mama, Bertram, and I somehow think that Oliver will soon be here so we can leave the lovebirds on their own if Mama will give her permission. Everything suddenly seems to be going right,' she smiled.

Philip was not convinced. 'It might be so for some, Sarah.'

She looked at him. 'Do not be such a wet blanket, Philip, come and let me tell you about Julian. You cannot be at odds with him for ever.'

'Very well, I suppose I must, if it pleases you, Sarah.'

'It does please me,' she said impatiently.

Sarah fetched a pelisse and bonnet and they walked together to the sea front.

The wind was blowing off the sea, but they stood together near one of the bathing machines. Swimming in the sea was enjoyed by some – even the Regent himself took a daily bathe – but the Wintersons had never been tempted into the cold water.

Philip stood holding Sarah by the hands and she laughed aloud at his expression. 'You are looking jealous again, Philip, but you must listen while I tell you Julian's tale, for it is most amusing.'

'I expect it is, Sarah, I cannot wait.'

'Philip, you are being rude,' Sarah said in a cross voice. 'Julian said that when they arrived in London, he went to see Crystal. . . .'

'Crystal? Good God, and what about the toothache?'

'The toothache? I do not think there was ever any toothache: I think it was an excuse to get you both out of the duel.'

'I suppose I should thank him, damn the man. And what is all this about Crystal? Do you mean James's actress – I was sure your cousin had been up to no good with her.'

'Philip Hesslewood, you are insulting Julian again and I will not have it. He has been very good to us and I am betrothed to him; you might not like it, but it cannot be undone. Now, let me tell you the story for it is quite the Canterbury tale. Julian had hinted to me that he might try to do something about Oliver and Hester, but I thought him to be roasting me. I imagined he had gone on a business visit, banker and tailor and the like for there is nothing in London in August.'

'And where does the famous – or infamous – Crystal come into it?'

'He had the idea that she might be able to put him on to a suitable husband for Hester.'

'But, Sarah, it does not make sense, Crystal is an actress,' objected Philip.

'Yes, I know that. Apparently she is appearing at Drury Lane at the moment, and she is well-known in the demi-monde of the city. He thought she might have connections with the type of gentleman he was looking for.'

'Sarah, my very dear Sarah, he has spun you a tale. Do not forget that it was Crystal who kidnapped Anita not so long ago. Julian would not have forgotten that.'

'I expected he thought that she owed him a favour; she did not get any kidnap money and Anita was quite unharmed.' Sarah suddenly did not feel sure of herself but persisted in her tale.

'You are besotted with the man,' Philip said harshly, joking no longer. 'You will not hear a word against him.'

'I will disregard that remark and will continue the story if you still wish to hear it.'

'I cannot wait to hear how Mr Julian Cleeve managed to secure Lord Cawcliffe for Hester Brewer; it all sounds most improbable.'

'Philip, whatever is it this morning?' Sarah asked.

'I do not like to hear you idolizing your cousin, that is all.'

'I shall take no heed of you then and will continue.'

'Yes, do, my sweet.'

Sarah glared at him; he was in an odd mood but she still wanted to tell him what Julian had done, so she took no notice of him.

'Julian took Crystal to dinner after the performance one evening and explained what it was he wanted – a titled gentleman who was on the look-out for a suitable wife. She said she knew several, so he parted from her hopefully and arranged to meet her two days later.'

'How much money did she want?' Philip was unable to keep back the words.

'Be quiet,' Sarah replied. 'He met Crystal again and she was pleased with herself, Lord Cawcliffe, she told him, and Julian was to meet him at Whites the next day. It seems the earl was made to measure; in his forties, widowed the previous year and keen to remarry. But he had no time for the young ladies who were introduced to him during the season; he wanted someone more serious. And, just listen to this, his estate marches with that of Sir Roderick Patmore who was married to a cousin of Mrs Brewer's. That was a bonus, Julian said.'

'I expect it was,' said Philip drily. 'And it all went according to plan?'

'Yes, it is too good to be true. Lord Cawcliffe presented himself at the Brewers' house and you know the rest.'

Sarah was now smiling happily, but she had the feeling that Philip was not pleased.

'What is it, Philip?'

He put his hands to her shoulders. 'I do not like the idea of you being married to a gentleman such as Julian Cleeve. In fact, he is hardly a gentleman, mixing with the likes of Crystal de Florette. I know I insulted him but there was some truth in what I said.'

'And what do you know of the likes of someone like Crystal if it comes to that?' Sarah knew she was being unbearably rude and she felt Philip stiffen.

'Are you trying to quarrel with me, Sarah? It is not the first time we have disagreed over your scheming cousin.'

'I am going to marry my scheming cousin,' she flared up at him.

'Not if I have anything to say in the matter,' came the sharp reply.

'It is nothing to do with you. Just because you were used to being as an older brother to me does not mean you can dictate to me now.' Sarah could feel herself getting both hot and angry.

'And what if your feelings tell you otherwise?'

'What are you saying, Philip?'

'This.'

And she was pulled roughly into his arms and he kissed her long and passionately. She could feel his strength, feel his desire and a tide rose in her body which desperately wanted to meet with him, to return passion with passion.

He suddenly let her go.

Sarah opened her eyes and became aware of her surroundings; the cry of the seagulls overhead, the roar of the sea and the voices of the visitors walking along the promenade. And her voice was shrill as she spoke to Philip.

'How dare you! To kiss me like that in front of all these people on Brighton beach. I want no more to do with you, Philip Hesslewood, and I am glad, yes glad, that I will be back with Julian soon – duel or no duel.' And Sarah rushed away from him leaving him staring miserably after her. I love her, he was saying, I know it now and I think she loves me, but all I have done is to push her further into the arms of Julian Cleeve.

Sarah shut herself in her room for the day, alone with her tumultuous thoughts; she did not even know that Philip had quickly packed his travelling bag, begged to be excused and had made his way back to Luttons Park in his curricle.

Sarah had to forget her quarrel with Philip for the next day they all returned to Little Cleeve. Marianne was to stay on for a few days as a guest of the Humphries; this arrangement was much to her delight.

Back in their small house, the first thing that Sarah did was to walk up to Cleeve Grange to let Julian know that they had returned and also to thank him for his efforts on the part of Marianne.

After her contretemps with Philip and the episode of the duel, she felt a little disquieted about meeting Julian again. She wondered if in fact that 'absence would make the heart grow fonder' – an old saying well known to them which she thought had come from one of the early poets.

But Sarah was to be disappointed. She found Cleeve Grange deserted except for Mrs Stockdale, Mrs Lingfield and the servants.

'Oh, Miss Sarah,' said a beaming Mrs Stockdale. 'I do hope as how you've had a good time in Brighton. It's been so quiet here without Miss Anita and Miss Marianne and the master.'

Sarah told the housekeeper about Marianne's betrothal to Oliver.

'Well I never. I've known Master Oliver all his life and a nicer young man you couldn't wish for. It was Lady Elizabeth who found me my place here, you know.'

Sarah smiled. 'I am glad she did, Mrs Stockdale.'

'But Miss Sarah, what about when you and the master are wed? Will you still want me?'

'I am sure we will,' replied Sarah. 'When are you expecting Mr Cleeve?'

'Any day now. He will be sure to come and see you the first thing he does.'

'Thank you, Mrs Stockdale. I will go back to Little Cleeve and see how the unpacking is going along.'

Sarah was glad to be home again and next day she was surprised when Philip, accompanied by Bertram, came on an afternoon visit.

In the drawing-room, Philip spoke to Sarah directly. 'Come into the garden with me, Sarah, I have to apologize to you.'

She did not want to make a scene in front of her mother and Bertram and followed Philip out of the room.

In the garden, he took her by the hands and succeeded in looking penitent. 'It is the same story all over again, Sarah, I have never been jealous in my life, but your Cousin Julian seems to stir up all the wrong feelings in me. Will you forgive my behaviour in Brighton?'

Sarah smiled generously. 'Of course I will, Philip, but I am sure I do not know how you will go on once I am Cleeve Grange and married to Julian.'

'Do not remind me, Sarah. I can still admire you from a distance. Now I want to be sure that you will regard me as a friend. You would come to me if you needed help in trouble, Sarah?'

'Yes, of course I would and thank you, Philip,' she replied. 'Are you still looking for trouble from my cousin, Philip, you do not really mean to fight a duel, do you?'

He grinned. 'It is up to Cleeve. It was kind of him to put himself out over Marianne and Oliver; I must regard him as a help-mate not a meddler.'

He pressed her hands lightly and they walked back to the house to join Lady Hadlow and Bertram who were discussing the plans for their wedding.

'I want it to be a happy occasion, Sarah,' said her mama. 'It is four years since your father left us and I do not think he would frown on a little celebration. . . .' She broke off as though listening to something. 'I thought I heard the sound of a carriage. Do you think that Julian and Anita have returned?'

Sarah hurried to the window to see a carriage which was strange to her; she wondered if Julian had purchased a new one while in London.

She was diverted by their maid, Nancy, coming into the room bearing a visiting card. She took it to Lady Hadlow and Sarah saw her mother frown.

'Mr Julian Cleeve? But he does not stand on ceremony with us. Why should he send in his card?'

Nancy was agitated and trying to say something. 'M'lady, it is not. . . .'

But Lady Hadlow cut her short, 'Bring him in, Nancy, I cannot imagine what all the formality is about.'

Nancy went out again and seconds later, in the doorway of the Little Cleeve drawing-room, stood a very tall, upright gentleman of about sixty years. His face was lined, his hair was white and he was looking around him with a curious expression on his face.

There was a fraught silence in the room; Sarah stared hard and grasped Philip's hand; Bertram rose with an exclamation on his lips; Lady Hadlow screamed 'Cousin Julian' and was lost in a swoon.

Bertram took charge. He rested Lady Hadlow back on the *chaise-longue* and gave the vinaigrette to Sarah, then he walked up to the stranger.

'It is Mr Julian Cleeve? I am not mistaken?'

The stranger spoke for the first time. 'You saw my card. Yes, I am Julian Cleeve. Is John here?'

Sarah took a step forward not understanding anything. 'But you are dead,' she said faintly and immediately felt foolish.

'Dead? Of course I am not dead. Can you not see that I am very much alive? Is John here? Did he tell you I was dead?'

'Who is John, sir?' It was Philip who asked the question.

'Who is John?' the gentleman echoed. 'Do you mean he is not here after all? I called at Cleeve Grange and asked for Mr Cleeve – I guessed that was where I would find him – but his housekeeper said that he had been in London and was expected back at any minute. She said I might find him here.'

A wavering voice was heard from the *chaise-longue* as Lady Hadlow recovered and stared at the visitor. 'You *are* my Cousin Julian, I remember you. You let the Grange to Lord Hadlow before you went off to America. Then you married our cousin Margaret, so we always called you Cousin Julian after that . . . it was all so complicated but I know you, Cousin. I was a young girl when you went away, but I married Lord Hadlow and we brought up our family at Cleeve Grange. When Julian . . . oh my goodness, he said you had died.'

And as if all this had been too much for her, she sank back with Bertram's arms to support her.

Sarah was clinging to Philip and was speechless. It was Bertram who spoke.

'You had better sit down, sir; it seems that there is a lot of explaining to do. I am Hesslewood from Luttons Park. You will have known the Hesslewoods. I remember you even though I was no more than a young lad at the time.'

The gentleman who said he was Julian Cleeve sat down and looked around him. 'Do you mean that my son has been calling himself Julian Cleeve? It is true that he was baptized John Julian, but he has always been John to me. Has he been living at the Grange?'

Sarah found her voice at last. 'Mr Cleeve, Julian and Anita have taken the Grange and Mama has come to live at Little Cleeve. I am Sarah Winterson and Julian and I are engaged to be married—'

Mr Cleeve was up again and towering over Sarah. 'My dear girl, you cannot be engaged to marry my son: he already has a wife.'

Sarah felt the room spinning and Philip jumped up and held on to her arms. 'Steady, my love, I will hold you and you will not swoon. Have courage, for I think we are in for some more shocks.'

Sarah swallowed hard and looked at Mr Cleeve. 'He told us that his wife had died and he decided to bring Anita to England to live at Cleeve Grange.'

Mr Cleeve had a heavy frown. 'Who is Anita? Another of his lady-loves?' It was as though he was speaking in disgust of his son.

Philip held on to Sarah. 'Leave it to me, just sit back in your chair,' he whispered. Then he turned to Mr Cleeve. 'I am afraid we are at a loss to explain any of this, sir. I am Philip Hesslewood, Sir Bertam's younger brother. We must try and come to some understanding. You must know that little Anita is Julian's daughter—'

But it was all too much for the older Julian Cleeve. He jumped up and faced them, his eyes blazing with anger.

'John has no daughter. I think he would have behaved differently if he had. Tell me about this Anita he calls his daughter. What does she look like?'

Philip replied quickly. 'She is a little thing, a very spirited little girl of about eighteen years of age. We all love her. She had been in a riding accident before she left America and had a slight limp when she arrived, but she has done well here. Sarah's brother, James – he is the young Lord Hadlow – persuaded her to start riding again. She has been in London with her father.'

Mr Cleeve was almost apoplectic with rage and had to sit down again.

'Annie Bell – that is who your Anita is. Annie Bell, the talk of Virginia and the best horsewoman in the state. Riding accident indeed; she was born with one leg shorter than the other, but it did not stop her riding and being one for the menfolk.' He turned to Lady Hadlow. 'I am sorry, Cousin, but I can only tell you the truth and a lot of it is not fit for the drawing-room.

'John is a wastrel and a libertine. He married Lucy Terrington, a very respectable girl, but she had no children. That was when he started his philandering ways with some of the young hussies in the state. Lucy left him, but she is still legally his wife. Then Annie Bell arrived on the scene and he set up house with her; he was already a gamester and lost heavily, but she made him worse. And eighteen? good little actress, that one; six-and-twenty if she is a day . . . well, what are you all looking at me like that for? You have got to know the truth even if it unpleasant.'

There were four of them in the drawing-room with Mr Cleeve. And each one of them was shocked and stunned, seemingly unable to speak. Bertram was still holding Lady Hadlow up for she looked as though she was going to swoon all over again. Philip was standing behind Sarah's chair and gripping her by the shoulders; her hands went up to find his and she clung to him.

'Why did Julian let us believe you had died?' asked Philip.

'Because we quarrelled, that is why; it was because I would

not let him have any more money. I am a wealthy man and I was forever bailing him out of his debts when he ran into Queer Street. I had said many times that I would not go back to England and would have to sell the estate. So, when I refused to settle an enormous gambling debt of his, we quarrelled and he and Annie were gone within the week. I expected him back at any time, but then I discovered that he had sold off part of my land without my knowledge and had gone off with the money. I made enquiries and found that he and Annie had sailed for England, so I put my affairs into the hands of a trusted friend and sailed after him and here I am. I guessed that he would have come to Cleeve Grange.'

He looked around him and gave a harsh laugh. 'You are perhaps thinking that I am a hard father, but I did all I could for John. In all honesty, he felt the lack of a mother in his life for Margaret died when he was born and I never remarried. I suppose I gave him everything he wanted to try and make up for his loss, but it was his downfall in the end. What is it? . . . Sarah, what did you say? Don't be afraid to speak.'

Sarah could keep silent no longer. She was still shocked, but she could not reconcile the Julian she had agreed to marry with the blackguard of whom Mr Cleeve was speaking.

'Mr Cleeve, Julian has been all kindness to us since he has been here. We have had our own difficulties and he has done his utmost to assist us; he is always most helpful and charming. . . .'

'Oh yes,' the older man interrupted. 'He was a charmer certainly, very handsome, polished manners, always out to please. If he had set his mind on claiming Cleeve Grange for himself and Annie Bell, he would have gone out of his way to be charming to his cousins and his neighbours.'

'But why would he let this Annie Bell, as you call her, pose as his daughter?' Sarah asked.

His voice softened a little and he smiled at her; for a moment,

Sarah could see Julian in him. 'My dear girl, John has been brought up in the knowledge of the ways of an English gentleman; for all I might have failed, I made sure that he knew how to go on in society. He would know very well that he could not take up a position at Cleeve Grange with his mistress at his side. You would accept his daughter, but not his mistress, am I right?'

Sarah nodded dumbly and rather forlornly. 'It is all very hard to take in, Cousin Julian – I suppose that is what we should call you. Anita took us all in, she even had my younger sister Marianne as her companion and the two of them are great friends. We did not suspect anything.' Then she felt Philip's hands tighten on her shoulders and she knew that he was reminding her that he had often told her of his doubts regarding her cousin.

He had told her of the early morning rides he had seen Julian taking with Anita and, as she thought of it, she had a vivid remembrance of small things which should have given a warning. The very first impression she had of him speaking rather guardedly until he was sure of her; his disconcerting ease with the dreadful Crystal; calling Anita 'Annie' and then saying that it was his pet name for his daughter; the intimacy of their embrace after the kidnap, and, most recently, her shock of Anita's words to 'John' in the kitchen, whom she had thought must be John Capel.

Now she knew Julian and Anita to be lovers and Sarah gave a little shiver.

'What will happen now?' she asked apprehensively.

Mr Cleeve did not hesitate. 'It would not surprise me if we had seen the last of the pair of them, though John must be running short of the ready. I doubt they will come back to Cleeve Grange if you say they have been in London a month, though they must have left clothes and possessions at the Grange which they would not want to abandon.'

He stood looking down at Sarah. 'I will sell Cleeve Grange

before I go back to America – it is my homeland now, as well as my livelihood. I am sorry if you thought you would make the Grange your home again, Sarah, I will hope for good neighbours for you. And what about my Cousin Mary? I remember you now.' He smiled at Lady Hadlow, his anger subsiding.

Sarah answered for her mother who did not seem capable of saying another word. 'Mama is going to marry Sir Bertram next month and she will move into Luttons Park. My sister Marianne has just become betrothed and will live in London where Oliver is a lawyer, and my brother, James, will also be in London. He is going into the diplomatic service. And I suppose . . .' she paused. 'I hope it will be possible for me to stay here at Little Cleeve.' She felt the pressure of Philip's fingers and thought somehow that Philip might have something to say on the matter.

Mr Cleeve looked from one to the other. 'I am sorry I have had to give you all such a shock. I apologize for my son's disgraceful behaviour and I must—'

But he did not finish as Nancy had tapped on the door and went over and said something quietly to Lady Hadlow who shut her eyes as though she could bear no more.

Nancy immediately turned to Mr Cleeve. 'Sir, a message has been sent down from the Grange to say that Mr Julian has just arrived back with Anita.'

Mr Cleeve jumped up. 'Right, let us go and confront them. I expect you will want to ask him a few questions, Sarah. You bring her . . . Philip, is it? And what about you, Hesslewood?'

Bertram did not hesitate. 'If you will excuse me, sir, I will stay with Lady Hadlow who is sadly shocked.'

'Into the carriage then,' said Mr Cleeve. 'My coachman will have it round from the stables.'

Philip pulled Sarah to her feet and steadied her. 'What about you, Sarah? Would you rather I dealt with it all?'

She looked up at him. 'No, I am all right now, it was just the shock. And I have a thing or two I want to say to Mr John Julian Cleeve.'

'Well done, Sarah,' said Philip, and lifted her hand to his lips.

In minutes, they were at the Grange, to find Julian's carriage at the front door and Julian himself hurrying from the house with a box and a bag under his arm.

When he saw his visitors, he hastily loaded his belongings into the carriage with a shout of 'Stay where you are, Annie.'

To Sarah, came anger and courage in a single second, and she ran forward and confronted Julian.

'How could you, how could you, Julian? To ask me to marry you when you already have a wife? And as for Anita, we all know the truth now. You pretended to act in our interests with Bertram and Mama, and with Oliver and Marianne, but it was to suit your own ends. And you never would have married me, would you? Trying to make us believe well of you when all the time you were wickedly scheming to deceive your own father, telling us he was dead and that he died of the drink. Indeed. . . .' Sarah was shouting by now, her voice rising to a high pitch and she lifted her arm and struck him wildly across the face. He pushed her away violently and she fell in front of him.

It was too much for Philip. He hit out hard at the imposter and the blow was so strong and heavy that the bigger man fell to the ground.

Mr Cleeve ran forward. 'Stop it, the three of you behaving like little children. Have you anything to say for yourself after cheating me out of a good piece of my land? What have you done with the money, John?'

Julian was on his feet again, but did not allow himself to be angry even after being hit by Philip. He maintained his smooth manner as he replied to his father, 'I have spent the money and, what is more, I sold the Grange while I was in London.'

'You have had the audacity to sell the Grange when it was my property?' his father raged.

'You don't need it, Father. Come into the house and I will tell you about it. A Colonel Linley has bought it; you will find him and his family to be excellent neighbours, Sarah.'

Philip took Mr Cleeve's arm and put a hand out to Sarah who seemed only capable of staring at Julian as though she had never seen him before. 'Come inside, Sarah,' Philip said. 'We cannot argue out here.'

But Sarah took no notice. 'Why did you say you would marry me when you knew your wife to be still alive?' she hissed at Julian.

'It amused me, Sarah, to get your mama and Bertram together and I enjoyed making Hesslewood jealous. . . .'

Philip moved as though he would strike out again, but Mr Cleeve managed to direct him and Sarah into the drawing-room.

'Calm down, both of you,' said the older man. 'It is myself who has the most cause for anger. Let John come and explain himself in a civilized manner.'

'Civilized?' muttered Philip. 'He does not know the meaning of the word.'

Inside the Grange, Sarah was listening for Julian's step across the hall, but what she heard was the sound of wheels on the gravel of the drive and she rushed to the window.

'They have gone,' she shouted.

Mr Cleeve and Philip joined her in time to see the carriage being driven at a spanking space down the drive and already they had reached Little Cleeve and were out of the gates.

'He has had the last laugh,' said Mr Cleeve. 'I should have known it. I imagine they had to remove all their effects before we arrived. It is no use wasting our energies on anger and recrimination. You are well rid of him, Sarah, and I will have to say goodbye to a wicked son who has caused me more trouble in the last twenty years than a whole family of sons and daughters would have done had my dear Margaret lived.' He looked at Philip and Sarah. 'I am going to have a last look at the Grange before I go. I will stay the night here and come and say my farewells to my Cousin Mary in the morning. Forget my son, Sarah, he has behaved badly but he has made his own punishment in that he will never have a settled life. Now you go and listen to what I think Philip Hesslewood has to say to you.'

He turned away from them rather emotionally and they heard his step down the passage to the kitchen and then his voice again. 'Mrs Lingfield, you still here after all these years? You have not changed a bit – we are all of us older. We must have a chat about old times.'

Sarah looked at Philip, her eyes brimming with tears. 'He is a nice old gentleman, Philip: how can a father and son be so different?'

Philip took her hand. 'Let us walk back to Little Cleeve and you can cry on my shoulder, Sarah.'

Immediately, the old Sarah was back. 'Cry? Cry over Julian Cleeve, I shall not shed a single tear for him. I feel very foolish, Philip, but certainly not sad on his behalf. I have never felt more angry in my life.'

'You can vent your anger on me, Sarah, let us step out quickly for you did not even stop to put on a pelisse or fetch a shawl. And we will sit on the bench in the wood-walk at the back of Little Cleeve and you can tear Julian Cleeve's reputation to shreds if you wish to.'

Sarah was glad to do just what he had said for she was not only feeling foolish, she was feeling very, very angry and was storing up all the names she was going to call the bogus Julian Cleeve.

It was late August and, by now, well into the afternoon. The sun shone but it had lost some of its summer strength though the day was still warm. Sarah sat on the bench with Philip and let the peaceful garden and the air cool her rebellious feelings.

Philip had his own ideas. 'First things first, my love,' he said, and took her into his arms and kissed her fiercely. They clung together and let their resentment at the behaviour of Julian Cleeve dissipate in their passion. Sarah's arms were around Philip's neck while his lips sought the softness of her skin at her bare shoulder. She shivered and it was with delight for never had she experienced such a wild throbbing throughout her body.

'Philip,' she whispered at last.

'I love you, Sarah.'

'What about Clara?' She had to ask the question.

'She is a sweet memory and we were very young. I do not come to you with a boyish love but with a man's passion, Sarah. It was Julian Cleeve who opened my eyes so I suppose that in a way, I should be grateful to him for he made me realize how much you meant to me. I could not bear to lose you to him and you know how jealous I became. That is how I feel. What about you, Sarah? Did you love Cleeve?'

Sarah was honest. 'I never did love him. I liked being with him and was soon won over after you and I had quarrelled.'

Philip sat upright with a sudden thought.

'What is it, Philip?'

'Sarah, shall we get married at the same time as your mama and Bertram?'

Sarah burst into laughter. 'But you have not even asked me to marry you, yet.'

'Oh dear, how remiss of me. Shall I go and ask your mama's permission?'

'Philip, now you are roasting me.'

'No, I am saying, will you do me the honour of becoming my wife, Sarah?'

'You cannot possibly want to marry me.'

'Why not?'

'Because of how I behaved with Julian. Also because I just

would not believe what you told me about him or heed your warnings.'

'I will forgive you for that,' he grinned. 'As long as you believe me when I tell you that I love you.'

'I cannot begin to imagine how you could possibly love someone who was so easily duped,' she shot at him.

'Are you always argumentative?'

She laughed. 'I was not always like this but Cousin Julian seemed to bring out the worst in me. I argued with him right from the start, as soon as he arrived at Cleeve Grange. Now I come to think of it, I called him our abominable cousin – I was not far wrong, was I? Do you know, Philip, I cannot think really badly of him.'

'I don't mind what you think of him as long as you think of him second and me first,' he taunted her.

'I will consider it.'

'Thank you, Sarah. I think I will try a little persuasion.'

'What do you mean?' she demanded.

Sarah was facing him. Her pretty cotton dress was thin and fitted closely to the body, the waist fashionably high, and the bodice tight. Before she had time to protest, he had slipped his fingers under the lacy edging of her bodice and sought her soft skin.

She gave a little shriek and pulled away from him. 'You cannot do that. We are not married and . . . we are out in the garden.' Her voice was high with the stir of excitement his caress had caused her.

His laugh was wickedly merry. 'I will do it again if you do not hurry up and tell me that you love me and will be my wife.'

Sarah looked at him and saw a Philip she could love; indeed she thought she must have always loved him.

'You are threatening me, but I will give in. Kiss me again, Philip, just to make sure.'

'Hussy,' he muttered, as he pulled her close and they were once again caught up in a long kiss.

'Well?' he said.

Sarah was breathless and certain. 'It is love, Philip. Perhaps we have always loved each other but it has only just blossomed.'

'And you will marry me?'

'I think I will have to, just to stop you behaving in an unsuitable manner in the garden.'

'Minx,' he said with great fondness. 'And you think we could have our wedding at the same time as your mama?'

'But it is only three weeks away, Philip.'

'I can only just wait for you for that long and it will give us time to call the banns.'

'You will not be serious,' she said. 'We have so much to talk about, but I think it could be arranged. I would like that, Philip, and I think Mama and Bertram would, too, both Hesslewood brothers being wed at the same time.'

'Shall we go and tell them now?' he asked her.

'No, we will not. I want to get rid of Julian Cleeve once and for all. He made a fool of me, you know, for I did like him. We were always arguing, but I liked it somehow.' Sarah's face wore a little frown.

'You can always argue with me if it makes you happy!'

'I wonder if we will? I know we quarrelled over Julian, but now I have to admit that you were right from the very first. You were always suspicious of him, why was it, Philip?'

Philip sat still with her hand clasped in his. 'I have to confess to not telling you the half of it for I knew that you would not believe me. I did not trust him, It was an instinctive feeling; I hardly knew where it came from. He was too smooth and calculating, arranging everyone's lives to his satisfaction, as though he was a little god. Then there were the rides with Anita. You thought I was mistaken so I could not tell you the whole, but one morning I had seen them stopped up at the wood and they were off their horses and embracing as though they were lovers. . . .'

'That is why you asked him how long Anita had been his daughter, I could not make that out at all.'

'Yes, and thinking back, I suppose it was the only time they had on their own. They made up the story of her not being able to ride to mislead us. He was very devious, your cousin, Sarah.'

'I used to call him devious and we laughed about it,' she told him.

'You were right. I expect he charmed you out of it.'

'I think he did. It makes me angry now the way he made me a pawn in his game. Yet you know, Philip, for all his faults, he did try and put things right for us; first Crystal, then getting Bertram and Mama together . . . wait though, I do believe he only asked me to marry him so that Bertram would turn to Mama. And it worked. I was pleased to have my mind made up about Bertram. Then he was very kind to Marianne and got rid of the frightful Hester.'

'He wanted you to think well of him.'

Sarah sighed. 'Yes, I expect you are right. And, Philip, to think he went to London to sell Cleeve Grange for the money to keep him and Anita – I cannot think of her as Annie – in prime style. I wonder what will become of them?'

'I do not suppose we will ever know. You will not grieve over it, will you, Sarah?'

'I will not,' she said with some certainty. 'I expect we will laugh about it all in years to come.'

'Give me one more kiss, my love, and then we will go and tell the whole Cheltenham tragedy to your mama and Bertram.'

'Mama will have the vapours again.'

'And Bertram will fetch the vinaigrette!'

And they both laughed as they made their way back into Little Cleeve.

They told the news of their engagement first and Lady Hadlow almost swooned with pleasure. Then came the rest of the story and the Wintersons and the Hesslewoods spent the hour until dinner-time tearing to pieces the character of the charming and scheming Mr Cleeve.